Plastic Surgery Confessions
Who Knew Sex, Drugs and Plastic Surgery Could be so much Fun?

PLASTIC SURGERY CONFESSIONS

Who Knew Sex, Drugs and Plastic Surgery Could be so much Fun?

Gail H. Bashara

12/14/19

To MY DEAR CHARLOTTE!

YOU ARE SO MISSED IN THE RADIO WORLD!

THANK YOU FOR KEEPING IT REAL IN THIS PLASTIC WORLD!

XOXO

Gail

Introduction

G abrielle Issad had learned long ago to only use board certified plastic surgeons. Her friend, plastic surgery mentor, and fellow Lebanese princess, Judy Gibran, now Houston's premier real estate Selling Super Star, had taught her that important lesson when Gabrielle first arrived in Houston from Gravestone, Oklahoma. At the time, Gabrielle had still been fresh and firm and hadn't yet realized what the years past twenty-nine would do to her body—she had just wanted the bridge of her prominent Lebanese nose to be a little thinner, the tip to turn up a bit more. She had met Judy in the waiting room of Dr. Barry Finkelstein, Judy's wide-brimmed black hat a stark contrast to the cool white-and-beige wallpaper behind her. Judy had been nonchalantly filing her nails, her plump lower lip stuck out in concentration, her Valentino–clad foot tapping impatiently. As Gabrielle would learn, Judy had been cut off from any further surgeries by Dr. Finkelstein—she already had the biggest, firmest fake boobs in town, and her face was stretched so taut she was beginning to look like a burn victim—but she still dropped by every so often to see if any new advancements in the field of plastic surgery could turn back the clock by even a few more minutes. And if nothing else, maybe she could slip out with another one of Dr. F's famed post-surgery swag bags that he gave to all of his patients as a little thank you—a glorious trove of discount coupons for Juvederm fillers, Latisse eyelash treatments, dermaplaning, chemical peels, and the always popular permanent make-up.

When Gabrielle walked in for her consultation, Judy had given her a warm smile, her veneered teeth sparkling. "Well, aren't you a doll? I'm Judy Gibran. I'm quite close with Dr. Finkelstein—I practically live here. In fact, I've got a cot back there, my very own room. The Judy Surgery Suite. And I'm only one procedure away from receiving a punch card for a free yogurt!"

When Gabrielle didn't answer, her eyes wide, Judy laughed. "I'm just kidding, Kitten, but I've spent enough money here that I should at least get a plaque on the recovery room's door. What are you here for? Lipo? Boobs? Cheeks?"

"Nose, actually—and that's it. Other than that, I'm pretty happy with myself," Gabrielle answered.

"Oh, Kitten, it's easy to be happy with yourself before you find that first wrinkle—or that first dimple where it shouldn't be. They don't stay in your cheeks, you know." She laughed. "Well, the cheeks on your face. And after you go under the knife that first time, there'll always be something else to fix."

After a twenty-minute chat in the waiting room, Judy slid her business card into Gabrielle's small hand—even Judy's well-manicured nails were fake and encrusted with tiny diamonds. "Let's have lunch," she had smiled. "I'll be dying to see your new nose."

Gabrielle hadn't been able to afford Dr. Finkelstein's prices right away, but meeting Judy turned out to be the turning point of her life. Now, almost twenty-five years later, they tried to have lunch every so often, just to catch up, and had seen each other through eighties big hair, nineties grunge, and finally into the polished and chic twenty-first century. Between them, they had also seen each other through several husbands (most of them Judy's), countless lovers of both sexes, and more than a few bottles of champagne and vodka.

While Dr. Finkelstein did Gabrielle's first nose job when she was still a young woman (twenty-two, to be exact, after years of painful saving on her part), after he had become quite successful but well before he had achieved a highly-esteemed status as a Plastics Magic Maker, there was no indication of how many more procedures she would undergo before reaching the ripe old age of forty-five. Even Dr. Finkelstein now had to confess that they had run out of body parts. Half jokingly, after undergoing two facelifts, three nose jobs, breast implants and a lift, and several extensive liposuctions, Gabrielle had suggested that Dr. Finkelstein invent a way to make her short legs a little longer, and perhaps to permanently whiten her teeth. Although the suggestions were made in jest, Gabrielle felt sure that Dr. Finkelstein regarded these comments seriously and, as one of the world's most renowned plastic surgeons, he would find a way to re-invent the medieval torture rack in order to lengthen her petite frame.

Dr. Finkelstein certainly considered it—they were experimenting with such leg lengthening surgeries in Japan—because such a fantastic new surgical procedure would certainly help with his expanding, excessive office overhead and his expensive, equally excessive Israeli-born fashionista wife, Areli. Even Areli's generous contributions to the arts and her annual, highly commended Thanksgiving Baskets for the Poor, assembled by her cook and distributed to thousands of hungry Houstonians, was paid for out of his pocket. He had no problem giving Areli all the surgeries she wanted, and she was certainly the envy of all the other doctors' wives (being married to a neurosurgeon just didn't have quite the same perks as being married to doctor who focused on plastics). But he was having trouble keeping up with her status as a member of "Wonderful Style World Magazine's Women to Watch" list and the Sak's habit that came along with it.

And the Barney's habit. And the Sakowitz habit. Her personal shopper from Neiman-Marcus was obsessed with sending her daily deliveries of the latest runway styles, and now that you could order anything you wanted online and have it the next day, they almost needed an SUV-sized mailbox to contain all the packages and catalogs that arrived daily at their door. Dr. Finkelstein (silently, as he wasn't such a fool as to say this to his wife) credited Areli's avid shopping with having driven their old delivery man into early retirement; he based this assumption partially on the fact that the new worker was a strapping young man of about twenty-two, with dark, dreamy eyes and muscles well suited to carrying a bronze five-foot giraffe statue shipped from Didier Romaine, the most prestigious antique shop in Paris, all the way up the long and winding footpath from their expensive, custom-designed driveway to their ornate front door. A faint glimmer of jealousy had briefly passed through the doctor's mind when he first saw the hot new delivery boy, but he quickly recovered, knowing Areli would never do anything that would jeopardize her hard-earned position in Houston society, or that would potentially result in the loss of his black American Express card. Besides, he had his own sexual affairs to worry about.

Dr. Finkelstein's five children, all attending Ivy League schools, were also a huge drain on his finances—especially Levi, in his sixth year at Harvard and still finishing up an undergrad degree in Expressive Sculpture, and who had only been there (sort of!) for the last five years courtesy of more-than-generous donations from his father. Compared to the other four children, sadly, Levi, was an overachiever. Add in the Finkelstein McMansion, of course located in Houston's most exclusive neighborhood, and Dr. Finkelstein's bank account was in the red more often than not.

While he didn't think he'd be making Gabrielle 's legs any longer, adding teeth whitening would be a breeze to tack on to his ever-competitive list of non-surgical, highly marked-up list of cosmetic enhancements, such as the ever-popular Botox, Restylane, and—the latest thing—anal bleaching. The women in a plastic city like Houston simply could not get enough of it, and it did give the occasional sex tape that leaked out in the PTA that extra Hollywood sparkle. Plus, to add to his financial drain, non-qualified surgeons and even dentists were now performing breast enhancements, facelifts, and sub-quality injections by the boatloads, taking business away from the more extensively trained and qualified members of the American Board of Plastic Surgery. Dr. Finkelstein was seeing a decided upswing in revision surgeries-badly botched boobs had paid for his wife's spanking new Bentley.

Dr. Finkelstein made a mental note to thank Gabrielle for the fabulous suggestions and perhaps even to give her a lower price on her next lip job—after he marked up the charge enough to cover the alleged "discount," of course.

The glittering world of plastics among the Houston socialite elite was certainly dog-eat-dog—but Dr. Finkelstein had no idea how brutal it could become…because while society is appropriately fawning to those on top, it's ruthless after the fall.

Part I

CONFESSIONS OF A
PLASTIC SURGERY ADDICT

Big Ass, Big Mouth, Big Nose

Gabrielle arrived in this world angry. As soon as she first opened her dark, lush lash-rimmed eyes to the world, taking in the weary doctor (who was a cousin from Sidon), her ecstatic parents, and the tacky dancing rabbit wallpaper of the Gravestone Obstetrics Ward, she let the world know exactly what she thought of it: by wailing for the first three months of her life. Other mothers dangled fat, giggling, red-faced babies in polyester onesies purchased at the Discount Dollar Store—but Gabrielle's mother shot the room apologetic looks as her own infant, clad in a white Italian cashmere blanket, snuffled and squawked and left streams of tears down the front of her frilly lace gown.

They couldn't take her anywhere without a cacophony of wails erupting—out to dinner, their friends' children's birthday parties, even to the grocery store for a gallon of milk. As soon as Gabrielle's mother, Martine, set foot out of the house and Gabrielle saw the wide Oklahoma sky and the miles of bleak, flat land, she would cry as if her heart was broken—and wherever they happened to be, heads would swivel, brows would furrow, and people would start to whisper about

9

what a frightful baby that Issad child was. The only thing that calmed infant Gabrielle was, oddly enough, a framed picture of nighttime at the Place de le Concorde in Paris, the streets filled with beautiful people and the exclusive shops glittering gaily. In time, her mother had photocopies of that picture everywhere—taped up to the car window, folded over in her purse, stuck inside the Nancy Drew books. And the preternaturally sophisticated Gabrielle, who started longing early for a bigger, better world, would gurgle happily, suck on her hand, and dream of being the princess who must live in the sparkling Louis Vuitton castle at 101 Avenue de Champs-Elysees. And more importantly, she was quiet.

Despite Gabrielle's surly disposition, her parents doted on her— their miracle child, the answer to their prayers, the salvation of their miserable marriage, and most importantly: proof that her father, Abraham Issad could actually produce a child. Although they hated each other with a savage, violent passion, her parents were Lebanese Orthodox Christians from the old world: an arranged marriage, where divorce was unacceptable. They spoiled Gabrielle and gave her all the love they were not able to feel for each other. Their nightly, loud, violent arguments made an impression on Gabrielle's soul long before she really knew what it all meant. To her it was a definitive measure of how not to succeed in marriage.

But as terribly as they treated one another, they treated their daughter as nothing less than a precious princess. Gabrielle's room was a sea of pink and lace, and she had every toy and book under the sun. The decor could best be described as "Lebanese Renaissance," with silk and tassels everywhere! As the only little girl in town with a subscription to the "International Doll of the Month Club," she would take it upon herself to lecture the other little girls about China, Peru, Spain, Portugal, Malta, and all of the other mysterious countries represented by the mail order collection. She was enrolled in ballet and tap dance classes at the nearby Tulsa studio of the famous Native

American prima ballerina, Maria Running Bear, before she could walk and singing lessons before she spoke her first words (which were, naturally, "GIVE ME!"). Only the best for the Issad's only child! So Gabrielle's anger lessened a bit as a toddler—after all, it's hard to be angry when you're having princess-themed birthday parties in the backyard for twenty of your best three-year-old friends and being showered with gifts such a glossy black Shetland pony named Midnight from Daddy.

However, by the time Gabrielle was nearing the end of elementary school, the old anger started to rise once again as she looked around at her world and found it lacking. She had saved her parents' marriage— so what? Who was going to save her from a horrible, vicious, arranged marriage with children who might turn out to be big nosed *B students?* It was unthinkable. Even though she had been born into a prominent Christian Lebanese family, she felt fate had dealt her an unfair blow. All of her smarter and wealthier relatives were fortunate enough to live in Paris, London, or Beirut, yet she was stuck in the land of red dirt, toothless farmers, and an inept educational system. How had she ended up in a frame house in Oklahoma, where she could see livestock out her window, when she longed so desperately for a romantic flat overlooking the Tour d'Eiffel? Her daydreams were filled with glamorous trips, couture outfits, and fabulous, exotic lovers, but her dismal, dreary days were filled with dirt roads, barbed wire fences, and avoiding 4H meetings. Raise a sheep? Can some corn relish? Bake a dewberry pie? The very thought!

Her charming, handsome father was the world's worst businessman and had quickly squandered his own inheritance—ruining any chance for his daughter to enjoy her deserved life of privilege and eventually leaving her to scrape up the money needed for piano and dance lessons herself (and of course such lessons were de rigueur for Lebanese princesses such as she—if she ever did get out of Gravestone, it would be a life-ruining humiliation not to have had them). Gone were the

11

barely-remembered days of lavish parties and a new dress for church every Sunday—now it seemed like the Issads were barely scraping by. Even though her father had been awarded the exclusive, highly-prized beer distributorship for the entire Gravestone County, he had managed to screw it up. How on earth her father could go bankrupt selling beer and liquor to alcoholic rednecks and Indians in Oklahoma? But after she sneaked a quick peek at his books one day she figured it out. Abraham Issad was apparently fond of giving his customers credit and then forgetting to collect the money. He felt like his customers were his friends, and he couldn't ask friends for money! *C'est la vie* was his attitude—but they weren't in France, and Gabrielle's own, more aggressive *carpe diem* creed didn't mesh well with her father's. She later found out that this trait ran in the family--her Great-Uncle Habib had been lavishly wealthy, but had ended up with only pennies because he loaned money to wheat farmers in his native Lebanon without collateral, and then let the farmers default with no penalty. Gabrielle knew she hadn't inherited this selfless gene. She charged her parents interest by the hour when they were late with her allowance, and if only her father had let her handle his books, the family might not have ended up firmly ensconced in the bourgeoisie.

Eventually Gabrielle's father lost the beer distributorship to others who were more willing to make their customers pay for their rowdy Friday nights with more than a hangover. Unruffled, Abraham went into the restaurant business with one of his brothers (owning his own restaurant was also a way to avoid Martine's terrible culinary skills), and that's when Gabrielle's life took a turn for the worse. Chubby and wearing her huge, coke glass–sized eyewear, she spent her afternoons playing with her Barbie dolls in the back booth of her family's "restaurant," a hamburger joint on Route 66 disingenuously named "The Hamburger King." She soon became tired of her rich black hair always smelling like beef grease, and she would dream of the day she could escape the pure torture of Gravestone. Even as a little girl, she

12

had known she was destined to live a different life, a different dream, and most definitely in a different state. Sure, there were people who knew the grown-up Gabrielle (or "The G Spot" as she would later be known in some circles) who would find it hard to believe she had ever touched something so plebeian as a Barbie doll—didn't she just have her maid play with her toys for her? And Gabrielle worked hard to foster this belief, portraying herself as a failure at anything remotely involving the risk of perspiration (other than Bikram yoga or ballet). No one would ever have guessed that to pay for her own dance lessons and Maybelline lipstick (horrors! Nothing but Chanel lip gloss for the Princess now!) she had worked afternoons teaching piano to Gravestone's rag-a-muffin five-year-olds and nights as the french fry technician at the Hamburger King, while maintaining a 4.0 average at the Gravestone High. After purchasing contact lenses, from yet another cousin who was an optometrist (if you were Lebanese you had more cousins than you could count, but at least they were good for a discount), Gabrielle got promoted and in her high school years could frequently be found taking short orders at the Hamburger King. Being away from the hot oil of the fryer machine cleared up her acne and whittled her waistline a bit, and she no longer followed her "two fries for you, one for me" system of filling cardboard cups.

Of course she found the beer and restaurant business in Gravestone less than inspiring. Sure, there was a certain clandestine appeal in the illegal gambling in the cigarette, cigar and Lebanese hookah smoke–filled dark back room at the Hamburger King, conducted weekly by her father and Gravestone's surprisingly large Lebanese community. Gabrielle would try to sneak back there as often as possible when the long distance truckers would pull into town—they were dirty and more than a little uncouth, but they had seen the country from California to Maine, and they were always willing to tell her a story about how things were in the big city. Still no dummy, she absorbed their crude yet fascinating tales with a grain of salt. Or Mrs. Dash.

Or whatever boring spices these poor, ignorant white people used. She knew that men wearing plaid work shirts and oil-stained jeans were not likely to be much of an authority on cosmopolitan matters, but her desperation led her to absorb every morsel of information on life outside of Gravestone she could find, no matter what the source! And although country music wasn't really her thing, there was an odd erotic charge about slow dancing with much older, sweaty men in the dim back room of the Hamburger King, where the jukebox wailed country classics such as Patsy Cline's "Sweet Dreams" while her father, uncles, and all of the other Lebanese men of Gravestone were too involved in their card games and backgammon to even notice.

Gabrielle's father, oblivious to the social order, didn't seem to see the incongruities between urging his daughter to play tennis at the country club (where his dues were, of course, always in arrears) and letting her work at the restaurant. But tennis whites and white aprons just weren't compatible in Gabrielle's mind. Instead, she sneaked out under the guise of leading a drama study group and headed to the black night clubs outside of town, where she could dance with loose abandon, smoke a little weed, and drink a little whiskey, all completely unsupervised. Fortunately, she had been drinking since age one at her father's distributorship (she and Midnight, the Shetland pony, had once even shared a frothy Schlitz) as well as at the Hamburger King, which was more popular than McDonald's in Gravestone by the sheer providence of serving beer and other, stronger, "off the menu" items. Tired local parents could have their own version of a very happy meal, Abraham Issad style!—an adult sippy cup that took the edge off. An additional result was that by the time Gabrielle reached her teen years, she already had quite a tolerance for the hard stuff. The bartenders at the black night clubs just outside the Gravestone city limits came to know the curvy Lebanese beauty well. They appreciated an enthusiastic, though somewhat clumsy dancer and they liked that she always paid in cash with rumpled up, damp dollar bills earned

14

from her tips at the Hamburger King, which she slowly, ceremoniously pulled out of her size 34D push-up bra—customers like her made it easy to cook the books a little. After a routine inquiry for "The usual?" they would line up several shot glasses of tequila with salt and lime. A few shots of this potion combined with Gabrielle's favorite vitamin, a nice little yellow-jacket diet pill, and she was off like a prom dress! There wasn't a club table in Gravestone on which Gabrielle hadn't danced (or a back room where she hadn't made out with whatever club patron was the lucky pick of the night).

However, despite her discontent with her lot in life, Gabrielle had learned at a young age not to complain to her father about the family's less-than-desirable geography and dwindling wealth. If she did, her father would tilt back in his chair, arms behind his head, a bottle of Arak shipped in from Lebanon via New York at his side, and pontificate with great feeling about his own grandfather. With his big, brown, gorgeous eyes growing misty, Abraham would recall how Gabrielle's great-grandfather and his five determined brothers had fled Lebanon to escape the horrors of the Ottoman Empire at the turn of the century. The Ottomans had occupied Lebanon at that time and had started forcing Christian males to serve in the Turkish army. Gabrielle's great-grandfather and great-great-uncles had traveled all the way to Oklahoma with not much more than the clothes on their backs during a time when Oklahoma wasn't even a state—it was Indian Territory, still a wild, desolate land of infertile red dirt. Abe would relate with pride how the Lebanese immigrants had first gained prestige and fortune by selling dry goods and scissors to poor Indians and indigent Scotch/Irish pig farmers and then had gone on to become fruitful merchants, a special talent that seemed to be genetically inherited among the Lebanese (well, any Lebanese man who wasn't her father). Finally, her father would wrap up his tale with how glad his own father was to have had finally produced a son after nineteen years and several daughters, and how he and Gabrielle's mother had finally been blessed with their own perfect little princess, Gabrielle, after years and years of trying. Gabrielle was not impressed with this story—she had seen pictures of her great-grandfather and his brothers, and they looked like an incredibly dull, boring group of stiff-suited men with huge noses who would have had no appreciation for the finer things in life. The women looked positively miserable. But then again, they were all grateful just to be in America, Home of the Free, Land of the Brave, whereas Gabrielle required a more specific, more sophisticated geographical location, one that she had only seen so far in Her Bible, "Vogue" magazine. She was seeking the "Land of the Bountiful" and the "Home of the Hedonistic," and damned if she wouldn't become one of its most prominent citizens. Plus, she didn't like to think of her parents "trying" for her over the course of years— her father's hacking cough from too much hookah smoke, her mother's not inconsiderable spare tire, and their propensity for knocking back a few cocktails in order to be able to do the deed made imagining such a situation too horrific. Gabrielle thought perhaps one of those nature channel specials on weird mating rituals in the wild might have been interested in the particulars.

Although Gabrielle inexplicably blamed her selfless mother (perhaps secretly jealous of any attention her father paid her mother, no matter how small) for ruining her chances of a life of leisure, Gabrielle loved her father with all her heart and soul. This meant she wanted to make her dashing, sweet, ineffectual, Daddy happy, she did—she really, really did!—but it was easier to be a Lebanese princess than a Lebanese angel, and the things he wanted were just so far removed from Gabrielle's shimmering dreams of high fashion, breathless jet setting, and torrid affairs. How on earth could he be complacent in a dump such as Gravestone as he taught his darling daughter every song in the the Paul Anka songbook, the amazing prose from "The Prophet," and the French, Arabic, and Spanish languages on the short drive to school? She didn't see how someone so cultured and worldly could be content in a place that valued moist cornbread more than classic literature. And so she rebelled. In fact, Gabrielle became quite accustomed to being in the principal's office during her high school years in Gravestone. Her legendary outspoken, politically incorrect behavior often resulted in reprimands from the school that had her parents shaking their heads in consternation—what had happened to their sweet little Gabrielle? They would never admit to themselves or anyone else that "sweet little Gabrielle" had existed only in their dreams.

Of course, all the other students would anxiously observe Gabrielle's misbehavior and delight in her subsequent punishment. If she had been friendly toward them, her exploits would have made her a hero in their eyes—a brave girl who stood up to the system and told it where to stick its erasers and algebra problems. But since she was just as haughty to them as she was to her teachers, they banded against her. Gabrielle lost recess all year long in third grade for telling the teacher she should really bleach her mustache or she'd be an old maid forever? *That's just what she deserved!* Gabrielle got kicked off the cheerleading squad for giving the football coach the finger when he asked how her teammates could possibly hoist her butterball rear into the air? *That's what she gets for being so uppity!* From the juvenile taunts such as "Hamburger Queen" to the more pointed "Ass-y Issad" and "Gabby Gabrielle" sneers—Gabrielle's reputation was leaving a legacy on bathroom walls from the Catholic kindergarten (where where she was an A+ student, of course) all the way to the nearest community college. The brutal spanking she received at Gravestone High School for writing steamy love notes (during--*yawn*--Algebra class) to her best friend's boyfriend was discussed for years afterward. Her hearty Lebanese posterior, covered on the day of her infamous paddling by a tight yellow daisy-patterned mini skirt, would receive Facebook likes for years to come. Though the balding, paunchy old principal would never admit it, it also fueled a few years' worth of his own fantasies—Gabrielle's tight thighs, her lacy white garter belt stolen from the closet of her cherished Aunt Lucille, the way the miniskirt molded itself to her firm young butt as she was bent over his large wooden desk—he shivered whenever he thought of it.

Truthfully, Gabrielle didn't care how many times she was spanked. She rather enjoyed it, actually. So what if she called the principal an imbecile, running a kangaroo court, a school full of hillbillies? It was true! She also pointed out that the school reading list was insulting and beneath her intelligence—she had read *Catcher in the Rye* when she was eleven, and furthermore thought Holden Caulfield didn't have a damn thing to whine about, being that he was wealthy and lived within a train's ride of New York City—but this comment only added extra vigor to the principal's next paddling, and she was becoming cognisant that his panting wasn't just the result of exertion.

Having been hardened by the bitter hostility between her parents, Gabrielle's defences had kicked into place at a young age. She easily learned to pretend to not care, to always block anything that felt like an emotion and make it go away, so as not to hurt. When she occasionally felt something that seemed to be a real emotion, she simply laughed it off, made a witty joke that made everyone else laugh, and then returned home to sob into her pillow. Her father had always dubbed her "too pretty, too smart," as he shook his head in hopeless desperation after each misconduct note from school. The family could have papered the dining room with all those pink slips, as her mother wryly noted after Gabrielle brought home three in one day. That was fine with Gabrielle. Cover the world with her pink notes! She *was* too pretty and too smart—for Gravestone. She'd fit right in in Paris, New York, Milan, Tokyo—the possibilities were endless. And she was pretty sure that she had learned how NOT to have a heart! Or to pretend, at least....

Gabrielle had a plan, and she knew her sassy determination, her quick wit, her intellect, and her lush Lebanese knockers would take her far in life. Precisely thirty-seven seconds after turning eighteen, she dragged two huge cardboard trunks, a fake ID and $756.38 from the Hamburger King cash register to the bus stop and left for Houston, where the shopping was excellent. (It was also the destination farthest from Gravestone that she could afford on a bus—a flight was entirely out of the question, especially since she had spent most of her savings from the Hamburger King on a fake ID.) There were a lot of Lebanese people in the garment business in Houston, which meant she could get some great discounts on fabulous clothes—and discount is a musical word in the ears of a Lebanese, creating a lump in one's throat and a tear in one's eye. First and foremost, though, she had some beauty maintenance to do. She had to have that huge Lebanese nose reduced—it had been the bane of her existence since she had reviewed reruns of "That Girl," starring the perfect little man-made nose of the High Priestess of American Lebanese girls, Marlo Thomas. How on earth would she get the money to pay for such a luxury?

Sex, Drugs and Rock 'N' Roll

When she first stepped off the bus in downtown Houston, clutching a suitcase full of everything she would need for her new life (miniskirts, lacy underwear, and six pounds of makeup and hair product), she looked around in fascination at the skyscrapers and the bustling men in suits. Here was where she belonged (even if she was disturbed by the way her thick hair immediately frizzed up into a monstrous cloud in the muggy, terrible humidity)—it was so full of life! Her heart pounding with excitement, within a few hours she had found a cheap walk-up near the Fifth Ward and talked the landlord into letting her have the first month's rent for free. Though she doubted that there were too many potential tenants vying for a building surrounded by junkies and homeless people, she wasn't afraid of them. They still made for a better view than the plains of Gravestone.

Now, on to the job hunt. Houston didn't really have a film or theater scene, so Gabrielle decided to channel her finely-honed dramatic skills into the next best thing: radio. And so what if she ended up working as a receptionist, making stale, instant coffee for the worthless salespeople, and low life advertisers, rather than being an on-air personality? She knew that if she only managed to sleep with the right people, she'd make it to the top through a careful combination of blackmail, wit, and charm. Plus, radio broadcasting had the three things near and dear to Gabrielle's heart: Sex, Drugs and Rock 'n' Roll!

Her parents had been disappointed in Gabrielle's choice not to go to college and major in something they considered "gender appropriate yet respectable"--perhaps interior design or home economics--leading to an equally respectable Lebanese husband, ideally a doctor or a lawyer, three to five children, and a big-ass house in the 'burbs. At first Gabrielle was tempted--partying for four years, with her parents condoning it? That certainly held a certain allure. However, she had soon decided it wasn't for her. She couldn't put her life off any longer, and besides, she had outgrown college boys in junior high school. She was going to shine like a star, and she didn't need a college diploma for that. Those four years were just opportunities for wrinkles waiting to happen. If she was going to be a success she had to start while she was still fresh and firm.

While interviewing at radio stations around Houston in her shortest possible crotch-length bright red mini skirt and highest matching platform heels, she came across Bubba Longview, a radio station owner who just happened to have a thing for Middle Eastern girls. Was it their creamy caramel-colored skin, their rich black hair, or their thrilling willingness to try anything in bed? He wasn't sure, but he was tired of the Chicken Fried Blonds in Houston and more than ready to introduce a little exotic spice into his audition couch. It turned out Gabrielle was just the spice he was looking for. And NO ONE could work a couch like Gabrielle!

As part owner of a small rock radio station in the Houston blue collar, industrial suburb of Pasadena, Texas, Bubba had wealthy, eccentric, and *clueless* partners from Pearland, Texas, who believed in low overhead. Bubba believed in a different kind of head, but as long as he didn't go over his allocated budget, his partners didn't question the excessive expense accounts and, more importantly, the steady stream of wanna-be personalities who were on air one day and off the next. A particularly enjoyable Friday morning ritual at KPDT was the "Free Tequila Fridays," where liquor brokers would drop off cases of the latest flavored tequilas for on-air sampling by the Morning Drive DJs. Fun, generous guy that he was, Bubba would allow the entire staff to sample the tequilas when the station was having a particularly good month (which was beginning to happen more often than not). It was also a great way to get the latest female addition to the sales department smashed before 10 a.m. This high-turnover position was most likely filled by a lovely young waitress with whom Bubba had been briefly smitten while cocktailing the night before. He inevitably lured her in with the immortal words: "Darlin', you, too, can have a high paying career in radio sales. Follow me back to mi casa for a cerveza and you can fill out an application and start tomorrow."

Dear Bubba had earned credibility with the owners years ago when they had jointly purchased an ice cream store, and Bubba had made the executive decision to immediately fire all the fat people--no customers wanted to be faced with the ultimate consequences of their own weakness for double scoops of butter brickle. His savvy marketing move resulted in the ice cream store becoming the most profitable chain in the area, beating out even Baskin Robbins, and any suggestion he made after that was golden and immediately granted—even for a radio station out in a desolate, undeveloped area near the Pasadena oil refineries in two double-wide trailer houses.

Random passers-by might have mistaken it for a good old-fashioned trailer park if there hadn't been a "Home of KPDT (as in "PasaDena, Texas!)" sign staked in front. Frequently, famous rock stars such as Billy Idol, George Michael, and Robert Plant would be limo'd out to the dusty, gray-graveled property for interviews--and the look on their faces was always the same: utter horror. Olivia Newton-John actually made a secretary disinfect a chair offered to her. But Bubba was proud of his radio station, and he had bigger worries than surly, spoiled rock stars. He was going to take his air waves to the top--and he wouldn't always be in a double-wide with stained wallpaper (and he didn't even want to know what those stains were). Though KPDT was still a small station, it was growing in stature thanks to Bubba Longview's aggressive promotion and business acumen, and was rapidly gaining national recognition for breaking new records and artists. Even the small-time, emerging rock stars turned their noses up at the location, but the publicity people insisted that this growing little rock station could ignite new careers and even help re-start the musical careers of aging artists. And they were right. Eventually the station would be turning stars away and even refusing the ridiculous demands of the more entitled ones (Bubba's infamous reply to a certain Latina diva: "You want only red Mike & Ike's in the candy bowl? Start pickin', honey, maybe you can get the job done before we go on air.")

For now, though, Bubba and his small crew were still stuck out in the middle of Nowhere, Texas. In one trailer, the sales and bookkeeping people officed (the Dull Trailer), while the other trailer housed the broadcast and production booths (the Fun Trailer). If you needed an invoice generated, you went to the Dull Trailer and helped the secretary dig through the neatly stacked files in the avocado-green bathtub. If you needed a little "pick me up," i.e. cocaine or diet pills, you went to the Fun Trailer. No one was ever turned away, and the Fun Trailer was the one reason many of the bigger stars would ever deign to be interviewed at KPDT in the beginning.

Even though Gabrielle wasn't impressed with the station's location, she needed a job and she was getting desperate. Cashiering at the Hamburger King, also known in the Gravestone community as

"Playing the Lebanese Accordion," was not helping on her resume. So when Bubba hired Gabrielle on the spot to do something called "traffic," she didn't think twice. Assuming she was going to be riding in a helicopter over Houston, Texas USA, with some cute sexy pilot, broadcasting live traffic reports and occasionally getting fondled while giving the scoop on rush hour, Gabrielle was thrilled beyond belief! She even went out and bought a sexy little navy slit skirt and jacket in case the pilot wanted to play the mile-high club. To her sad dismay, however, she learned that "traffic" was a boring, dull desk job that consisted of scheduling radio commercials. She spent her first day despondent at her desk, her dreams of titillating KPDT listeners with her husky laugh and innuendo-laden traffic reports dashed. ("We have a REALLY BIG THREE WAY jam up on 610. Several people got REAR ENDED. This is going to be SLOPPY AND MESSY and we'll have to send in a REALLY BIG CREW of SWEATY FIRE FIGHTERS TO CLEAN IT UP.")

Once again, Gabrielle was angry. As she sat at her dirty little pathetic vinyl desk, which wasn't even in the Fun Trailer, she would peruse the advertising contracts and add up the commissions the lazy, lousy salespeople were making. Knowing she was--as always!--smarter than everyone else, not to mention wildly more charismatic, Gabrielle began to search for a way to get into the (much) higher paying radio sales department. If she could get into sales, it could pay for her much-needed nose job--and she was sure her nose was the only thing holding her back from moving onwards and upwards (perhaps upwards in a traffic helicopter). She consoled herself with the fact that every hour she spent riding around with Bubba in his brand-new Lincoln Continental with the fake convertible top, taking legal pads full of copious notes of everything he said and did as a guideline for her own success, couldn't possibly be time wasted. She was learning more about success from him than she ever would have from the fat red toothless frat farm boys she would have dated in college in Okla-fricking-home-a.

Gabrielle knew that her first step was to get out of these trailers located near the filthy oil refineries—and since she couldn't find a better job, she'd decided to make KPDT go instead. She was sitting seductively in Bubba's lap on one sticky, humid, Pasadena summer day, playing absentmindedly with his earlobe--the first thing she bothered to find out about men was what made them putty in her hands, and Bubba's earlobes were the key to never hearing the word "no"--when she made her move.

"Bubba," she purred. "KPDT is getting too big for this trailer. We've already won several national awards, including "Billy Board's" Best Rock Radio Station to Watch." Have you ever thought about moving us somewhere--how do I say it nicely--other than the middle of fucking nowhere?"

Bubba thought a bit before answering--he was a man of few words, which was something Gabrielle appreciated. She hated chatty men, unless they were queens. "I've checked out a few spots in Port Arthur, home of the late, great Janis Joplin, but nothing promising yet. I'll just have to keep looking, though--the investors really like the idea of relocating there because real estate is so cheap." Disgusted, Gabrielle pulled back, her fresh, young, still-untouched face disgusted. "PORT ARTHUR? Darling, that's a cowtown. Space City is where it's at. That's where the stars want to be. That's where *I* want to be. Every lunch and every dinner would be a par-tay--and you know how fun I am when we all get liquored up. Plus, we'd get to play with the Big City Advertising Power Brokers!"

That did it. Bubba wasn't exclusively attached to Gabrielle, and he currently had his eye on Yasmine, the station's curvy Persian cub reporter--she had just been named "The Sexiest Woman in Texas" by *"T as in Texas!"* magazine, and he was ready to name her the sexiest woman on his couch. Moving would be just the way to get distance from the greedy, smothering Gabrielle and give his station (and social life) the prestige and boost it needed. So, after much

24

prodding, Bubba's anonymous investors agreed to move the radio station from the trailer houses out of the country and near downtown Houston, the hub of all the major Southwest advertising agencies. The ad community was famous for excessive drinking, drugging, and anonymous sexual encounters, so this new location would serve Bubba and his employees well! Better yet, a shorter drive home from the bars would cut back on those expensive jail bailouts he frequently had to cover for his staff. He thought fondly back to the last office party held at his house--the cases of champagne, the cocaine freebasing, and the excessive nudity. Yasmine had taken off all of her clothes and slid down the slide at his pool--with one leg straddled on each side. She had entered rehab shortly thereafter at the insistence of her horrified lover, Sasha, her former stylist, and was last seen interviewing one of the stunt doubles from the movie, "Porky's Revenge III"--finally sober but much less entertaining.

Gabrielle was eager to step into the reporter's Fuck Me Pumps (and her salary and expense account), or perhaps a career in sales, but with her limited radio experience she was still shut out. But she didn't let that get her down--at least they were moving to Funky Town! Soon her whole life would be the Fun Trailer—and after almost two decades of drudgery it was high time she got the glamorous life she deserved.

Judy Gibran

As Bubba pored over real estate listings one sweltering Friday afternoon, Gabrielle walked by and dropped Judy Gibran's business card on Bubba's desk. The thick, creamy white square fluttered from her fingers, landing right in the middle of his "Advertising Agenda" weekly newspaper. "Judy Gibran, Real Estate" was emblazoned on the front of the expensive card in bright pink, swooping letters. "Why do for yourself what you can pay others to do for you, darling?" Gabrielle asked. She had remembered that she had Judy's card when she had gone back to Dr. Finkelstein's office a second time, wheedling for a deep discount--but he hadn't budged, and she still didn't have the perfect narrow nose she'd always dreamed of. She just couldn't afford it--and that's why they needed to get out of these godforsaken trailers and into the big city. But maybe, if Judy made a nice profit off this transaction, she'd give a little kickback to Gabrielle--and Gabrielle would take that straight to Dr. F.

Bubba was familiar with Judy's name and reputation, but before he could even agree Gabrielle had called and made an appointment. Now that she had been promoted from the dismal traffic job in The Dull Trailer to Bubba's personal assistant, she had his Rolodex, access to his personal red-hot line phone, and a lot more power. Whenever he wasn't looking, she copied a few of the best contacts for herself, and she now had quite an extensive list of hot, hot, hot music celebs, their agents, and behind-the-scenes music money makers at her disposal. She wasn't sure what she was going to do with them, but she knew they would come in handy someday.

Bubba wanted to find the property himself—he had never trusted that realtors wouldn't steer him toward overpriced properties while hiding the cheaper ones in order to keep the profits rolling in their own bank accounts. However, the A/C was again on the fritz, meaning that everything was covered in a thin sheen of humidity and that more sweat was running down their noses than fun white powder was going up it. The cheap plastic box fans just pushed the hot air around and blew files out of the bathtub, and some of his best employees were threatening to permanently jump ship if he didn't either get a new unit installed or institute a more casual dress code—perhaps one allowing cut offs, halter tops, and flip flops. He knew he didn't have time to go property hunting on his own if he wanted to keep his team from roasting alive in the trailers, and so eventually he gave in—once again—to Gabrielle. (Even though he wasn't sure she deserved it--he knew she was stealing his contacts and who knew what else).

The following Monday, Judy Gibran re-entered Gabrielle's life like an Oklahoma tornado. Driving up to the trailers in her Cadillac convertible luxury automobile with gold customized hubcaps bearing her initials and her office phone number (always gotta advertise and sell, sell, sell!) and wearing head-to-toe diamonds, Judy represented everything Gabrielle wanted to be. Judy was already a legend in Houston--not only for her real estate savvy, but also for her over-the-top, sparkling lifestyle. Judy's draping diamond extravagance primarily consisted of little bumblebee-themed pendants, pins and rings. Even her pet chihuahua, Francisco, who rode everywhere with her, wore a little diamond-studded collar. More important than the car and the diamonds was something only another Lebanese woman could understand: Judy had the smallest, most perfect nose and glorious knockers even larger than Gabrielle's. Upon their first meeting, Gabrielle had gasped aloud with envy--and she still dreamed about that perfect little nose on her own face.

As the premiere high rise and commercial realtor of Houston, Gabrielle knew Judy was the perfect salesperson to find a new home in Houston for KPDT. As Judy sashayed up to the trailer door, oversized Louis Vuitton bag under her arm, Bubba's taste for Lebanese women came into play and he was practically drooling over her hand. Gabrielle knew that they'd be moving to town within the week--one good false eyelash flutter from Judy would have them in the nicest high rise office building in Houston.

"Nice to meet you, Sugar," Judy purred after she and Bubba had been introduced. "And you are a handsome man--just like Gabrielle said!" She gave a tinkling laugh. "You're wasting those good looks out here in the boonies, baby." Gabrielle laughed, too, though she had said no such thing--she thought Bubba looked like a sunburned rhinoceros, and his halitosis could peel paint. She didn't know how she'd managed to keep him at bay for this long, but then again she was a determined girl and could do anything when she put her mind and her twat to it.

As Judy kept up the friendly chit-chat, both Gabrielle and Bubba

Longview were paralyzed with awe, their little eyes bouncing as wildly as Judy's cleavage. Within a few minutes she had ushered them into the car (the chihuahua still in the front seat, of course), and the six of them (Judy, Bubba, Gabrielle, Francisco, and Judy's two amazing knockers, which really needed their own seat belts) drove off in the fabulous golden Cadillac to search for office space for KPDT.

Gabrielle turned out to be right about the speed of their move--all Judy had to do was lean across the desk showing her ample cleavage, wrinkling her pert little nose, and Bubba signed on the dotted line. Their new address was on the fabulous Westminder Street, and they would finally have real file cabinets to store the invoices--not to mention actual offices and mini blinds that conveniently worked. Gabrielle and Judy had lunch the next week to celebrate--on the company card, of course.

"Gabrielle," Judy slurred, waving around her sixth glass of champagne, "the first thing you have to do is lose weight. In your hips *and* in your nose--why hasn't Dr. F fixed you up yet? You'll never get someone better than Bubba until you do some maintenance work!"

Gabrielle wasn't offended--she and Judy were on the same page. "I know. I can't afford it yet. I've been saving, but it's hard when you're alone. I can't eat and have a roof over my head *and* get my nose fixed."

"Well, I've already told you that you need to eat less," Judy said. "That baby fat's not doing you any favors. And you need to get someone else's roof over your head, Kitten. I spent my twenties under all kinds of roofs—lovers and husbands--and by then I had enough to buy a condo, a great pair of boobs and my baby the customized El Dorado. And I haven't needed a man since--but I know quite a few of them. And by know I mean slept with. We'll get you fixed up in style, Darling."

New Nose, New Girl

The first part of getting fixed up in style was a new nose and finally getting that hard-earned promotion into sales at the radio station. The increase in pay, along with a healthy kick-back from Judy's commission on the KPDT move and yet another station credit card, had Gabrielle in Dr. F's office and under the knife within a month. While the initial bruising and bandages were an unsightly shock, Judy threw her a big reveal that was worth the month of ugly--and Gabrielle almost cried when she saw that perfect, pert little nose on her own face. Except for the few decades between them, she and Judy could have been sisters.

Her parents cried on the phone after they received the picture she sent them and asked why she had ruined her precious, perfect face? Gabrielle knew they would get used to it—even though her mother claimed to not recognize her any longer and said she couldn't possibly open the door for a stranger for Thanksgiving dinner. But Gabrielle hadn't planned on going home for Thanksgiving (or any Thanksgiving, ever, especially now that the family feast consisted of burgers, fries, and artfully arranged individual ketchup packages instead of turkey and stuffing). Anyway, she knew that perfecting her face was the key to happiness—and now that she was so confident there was no stopping her.

The second the last bruise was light enough to be covered with concealer, Gabrielle's new nose started taking her far in life. For a while, every day was a whirl of parties, expensive restaurants, and meeting Judy's wealthy clients and friends. Every meal was a banquet and every night was awash with endless glasses of champagne— usually pressed upon her by some admiring man who just couldn't wait to tweak that adorable little nose (and various other parts of her body). Drug dealers on all the disc jockeys's speed dials, three-martini lunches, and doing blow off the asses and nipples of strippers was just another day at the office in radio sales! However, all of those expensive meals, courtesy of a never-ending stream of boyfriends and girlfriends, packed more than a few pounds onto Gabrielle's petite frame. She tried to ignore it, but after bursting the top button off her YSL blouse (bought on Bubba Longview's business credit card!--didn't work clothes count as a business expense?) and almost putting out a date's eye, she started to get a little worried. It now seemed like every day was Fat Tuesday…and Fat Wednesday, and Fat Thursday. After having a nightmare that Weight Snatchers had printed a poster with her portrait and the word "WANTED" scrolled across her rear, she immediately lost twenty pounds.

She also decided it was time to start giving back--maybe a little good karma would keep that extra weight off her hips. Her generous, hard-earned sales bonuses were often mailed straight to her parents in order to help out their now struggling, tired, out-of-date Hamburger King. The competition from the new WalMart, which featured $1 hot dogs, was killing their business. Sending cash was much easier than having to step foot in Gravestone and confront all those sad ghosts of her chubby, near-sighted past life, and she didn't have to waste any vacation days. In order to prove herself as not only an enthusiastic taker, but a giver, she also started providing annual anonymous scholarships to her beloved Running Bear Ballet Academy, a dance sanctuary where she could escape her youth in Gravestone. With help from Bubba Longview, who needed some evidence of community service for the KPDT's public files for the FCC, Gabrielle even instigated a tornado watching service for Oklahoma's AM radio stations, creating a network of weather information that saved property and lives. As she achieved her own social status and financial independence, she found it less necessary to put up the hard shell around her vulnerable heart, and she came to enjoy being generous as she climbed the ladder of success. Her love of literature found her reading books to the blind (*Valley of the Dolls* was a favorite), and she often marched for pet's rights. Well, she actually only made it to one march, but her housekeeper, Consuela, was better at outdoor sports and often showed up wearing Gabrielle's name tag at the events. And though Gabrielle's subsequent donations to the SPCA helped launch an aggressive pet chip identification program in Houston, she was not deterred when her ideas for an animal massage center and a yoga for pets class were less well received--not everyone was as forward thinking as she was! Another failed social services activity attempted by Gabrielle was as a volunteer for the Houston Substance Abuse House. Showing up with a hangover after Free Tequila Friday at the radio station, Gabrielle was short on sympathy for those who could not control their substance intakes.

The new nose and the new trim hips, as well as Gabrielle's growing reputation as an eccentric community volunteer, caught the attention of an Egyptian businessman who lived in Cairo but kept a condo in Houston, the American home office of the Egyptian consulate. They bumped into each other in the KPDT office building elevators. Gabrielle was sneaking back from a trip to the bar at the nearby La Palma with the secretary, who was very nice but would never meet someone unless she did something about those furry, wild eyebrows and buck teeth. Salaam Abdullah was rushing to a big important meeting at Goldman Sachs. Though he was much older, Gabrielle was immediately drawn to his distinguished salt-and-pepper hair, his immaculate, custom suit, and his fat wallet full of premium credit cards. Within the hour, she was sneaking back to the bar with him, and their courtship became the stuff of legend. He showered her with furs and jewelry, filled her office with orchids and roses, and sent her and several of her girlfriends on a special spa week in the Hamptons (turns out Gabrielle had a lot more "girlfriends" than he thought! Especially when you included her best gays, Ike and Darrin, whom she had met during a wild night in the Meat Packing District during her senior trip). Best of all, because he didn't live in Houston full time, this left Gabrielle to sleep with whomever she pleased while

31

he was gone. And in the radio world, the opportunities were endless!

Good old Bubba Longview didn't react jealously--he had recently decided he also had a penchant for redheads, and there just so happened to be a fiery little number (nicknamed, appropriately, "Red") interning during middays in the control room. Plus, he was glad that there weren't any more mysterious charges on his business expense card--he was embarrassed that he didn't remember going to some place called The Lost Time Tavern with Nick Nolte, who was in town to promote his latest B movie, but then again he did drink a lot, and he wasn't as young as he used to be. The alcohol, combined with all the uppers, the downers, the in between-ers, the grass, the coke, the acid, the ecstasy, the horse tranquilizers, the magic mushrooms--all these things just to keep up with Judy, Gabrielle, Yasmine, and all the young DJ's and music reps--had left him bloated, exhausted, and more than a little gray. He would be the first to wish Gabrielle congratulations when Salaam solemnly popped the question, down on one knee and his eyes shining with love for the high-spirited Gabrielle.

Salaam's proposal was lavish, involving an elephant and a four-carat canary diamond. Gabrielle loved him the best she could - she really, really did! - but the perfect wife she was not to be. She came to realize that what she truly loved were the lifestyle enhancements he could provide. And she was pleased that Salaam didn't ever press her to give up her career. Unlike many conservative Arab Christians, he didn't mind her working. In fact, he encouraged it! Free concert tickets with VIP parking passes, front row seats at all the movie premieres, backstage passes to the hottest rock concerts, complimentary limos and meals and never having to wait in line for anything!--all these things appealed to his ego. It made him sound more important to his friends, and he liked to be the forward-thinking one among them. So what if his wife worked? It made her happy to "play" at success, and her happiness was the most important thing. She was so cute with her little commission checks!

Within three months, they were married--Gabrielle may have been sleeping around, but not with Salaam, and he refused to wait any longer for his blushing bride. Six hours after the ceremony and hundreds of gallons of champagne later, Gabrielle was throwing kisses out the back of a stretch white limo, tightly corseted into a dress with so many layers of silk and lace that just the skirt could have filled a city block. Their first honeymoon stop was Cairo, where Gabrielle got a less-than-warm welcome from Salaam's tiny, beady-eyed mother, who saw right through Gabrielle's little act. Before the happy couple left, Salaam anxiously asked his mother what she thought of Gabrielle. Mamma said simply, "Crooked as a barrel full of snakes." But Mamma always had been jealous of every girl her baby son brought home, and he brushed her comment aside. It was nothing compared to what she said about his elder brother's Tunisian wife. Soon the eager young couple were dining at the best restaurants in Monte Carlo, strolling through Bond Street in London, and storming the Left Bank boutiques in Paris. Gabrielle was happier than she ever had been, and her parents were thrilled with her, too! Finally, they thought, she had landed a good catch and could stop working and make herself respectable by producing a fine line of dark-eyed little sons. Or so Gabrielle's family, Salaam, and his mother fervently hoped, though they all secretly doubted Gabrielle would be so easily tamed.

However, when the honeymoon ended and the Abdullahs had unpacked in Salaam's trendy downtown condo (found for them by Judy, of course-yet another kickback for Gabrielle), reality trickled in. So did the credit card bills--it turned out Gabrielle had quickly run through Salaam's entire fortune, her chump change from the radio station, and then some. Soon enough he was working around the clock just to keep out of the red, because, of course, Gabrielle couldn't cut back her lifestyle. She might as well just move back to Gravestone and sling burgers alongside her fat, hairy cousins! It would be a death sentence to have to shift her taste from Givenchy to Gap. However, in her own little way, she did come to love Salaam and managed to settle down for a few years. Sometimes she even cooked. Well, she didn't actually "cook" in the technical sense--she ordered Chinese and then had the maid set it out in her Christophe china, but it was close enough. Salaam never quite understood why his little Lebanese wife was so adept at whipping up egg rolls and stir-fry instead of hummus and stuffed grape leaves, but he always smiled at her appreciatively and ate with gusto (despite the later indigestion from all that MSG). Gabrielle had her doubts--perhaps she could have done better--but the wild sex with Salaam had shut up the little voices of discontent in her head for a while. They had done it everywhere from the pyramids to the KPDT control room, and the things he could do with his tongue took her breath away and made her toes curl. Even her naked acrobatics on a swing in a certain rock star's apartment hadn't been this exciting!

It looked like she finally had everything she wanted--the perfect nose, a wallet full of credit cards (most of which she didn't have to pay off herself), and a husband who adored her. What could go wrong? And how could she possibly want more?

Old, Fat and Bitter

Of course, even the most ecstatic of new marriages slowly mellow out into complacency (or, more likely, explode into mutual dislike and recrimination). The husband stops bringing home small gifts on anniversaries, and the wife begins shaving her legs only on special occasions. The Abdullahs' marriage was no different. The once dashing, older, romantic Salaam had turned into Grumpy Grandpa, constantly complaining about his aches and pains and not being fun at all. He was constantly harassing her to "Turn down that loud music!" She could hardly get him out of the house to attend rock concerts anymore, not even to see Tom Petty.

34

Gabrielle's best gay boyfriends, Ike and Darren, had long ago warned her about the Wild Mountain Beaver turning into a Lame, Tame Possum. Unfortunately, the possum had turned into Road Kill. When Ike and Darrin would drive down the freeway past the Bad Adventures condos, they would remark: "I know there's a little girl up there in that high rise just dying to get out!" Gabrielle didn't feel sexy, she didn't look sexy, and she didn't act sexy. Judy had known something was up when she caught Gabrielle—without make-up—at the gourmet grocery store, wearing a pair of Uggs and a faded, tattered, old KPDT T-shirt, hand autographed by A Flock of Seagulls. Gabrielle was almost unrecognizable without her false eyelashes and signature glossy pout, but Judy knew it was her when she saw her cart full of tabouli, hummus, and seven huge packages of pita bread. All the other expanding, run-down, desperate middle-aged women were sensibly buying low-fat potato chips and chardonnay by the cases (known as the "River Stokes Diet").

Judy tried to stage an intervention, booking them a spa day and an appointment with the Neiman's personal shopper, but even an armload of Dior couldn't salvage Gabrielle's mood. All the years of boozing, drugging, Lebanese food, and show biz had finally caught up with her. That cracked wheat could really bloat a girl. (So could the greasy take-out from Taco Tom's, which was always delivered by that divinely cute delivery boy, Timmy...FABULOUS full service. Another great recommendation from Judy.) Oh, sure--her precious career in radio sales was remarkably still going great, and she could finally buy almost anything she wanted--without hiding the receipts from her husband and pretending she'd had it for years. ("This old thing? Darling, you never pay any attention to me--I wore this twice just last week." Or, "I just picked this up from the dry cleaners. I forgot it was even there--they were just about to send it to Goodwill.") However, she had to confess that her success at the station couldn't bring back her youth, and she was now certainly among the oldest in that young person's profession. Those little twenty-four-year-old blond, skinny bitches, vying to take her place--why, she ate two of them daily for lunch! She comforted herself with the thought that they could never have competed with her lush curves, killer instincts, and alluring sexuality when she was in her heyday (she also comforted herself with chocolate truffles and Grey Goose, her vegetarian diet, which, although satisfying, was in itself a problem).

Her fading youth wasn't the only thing dragging her down. They had no longer been able to keep up with the mortgage on their condo downtown and had been forced to move into another of Salaam's properties: the Bad Adventures condos on the seedy side of the city. He had purchased the building during the financial crisis of the eighties, thinking the area would later develop and he could renovate the building to attract wealthier residents, but he had ignored the the inspiring and prophetic words of the Great Realtor, Judy Gibran: location, location, location. The Bad Adventures condos had none of those three requirements, and daily the structure and value of the building were dimpling and falling as fast as her ass. Gabrielle was sure the tacky, dated popcorn ceilings were emitting freaky, mysterious, poisonous fumes. Judy had told her not to buy there, and even Judy's real estate genius couldn't sucker in another buyer to take it off their hands. It was just down the street from a strip center featuring the tacky, unfortunately named "Chateau de Coif" hair salon, and Gabrielle would rather shave her head than get a cheap haircut. Unfortunately, this was feeling all too familiar: Had she married the world's second worst businessman? She had always had a thing for daddy figures, but this time perhaps she had gone too far. Depressed, she was soon sleeping pretty much around the clock. And alone. (Well, perhaps warmed by a nice little non-caloric portion of mother's little helpers.)

After a particularly large bonus, things had looked up for a while, and with their bank account running over with excess zeros they had just sublet their condo at the Bad Adventures and had moved into a beautiful, sleek modernist-minimalist River Stokes penthouse, once featured in "Architecture Houston " magazine, facing the glorious skyline of smoggy downtown Houston. Despite her expanding waistline, Gabrielle was happy there--she was sure the customized decor including the luxurious white carpet, the floor-to-ceiling windows, and the skinny mirrors in her enormous marble Jacuzzi bath took inches off of the appearance of her thighs. But Salaam's fortune had never recovered from her wild spending on their honeymoon, and once again they blew through the small amount of cash he had recouped. Then came the worst day of her life: they were forced to move back to the Bad Adventures, where their only view from the sad second floor (alas- not the penthouse) was of the drunken Greek soccer fans at Parthenon Bar and Grill. To add insult to injury, they had to pay the tenant subletting their old place a fee to move out early—which he willingly did, though he left behind mysterious used syringes, cigarette lighters, and aluminum foil, as well as an unpleasant, lingering odor from his obsession with cooking authentic, curry-based Indian dishes.

When they had first moved out there a few young couples were living in the building, the rundown property now housed nothing but grumpy old people, which made Gabrielle feel even older and grumpier. The place was a virtual death trap, and ambulances circled the building in fifteen-minute increments. Forget Florida—there was no doubt that **this** was actually God's waiting room. Gabrielle was sure the pores of the sad old building breathed death--and every time she looked at the stains in the dark hallways (she had thrown an overripe avocado at Salaam during a particularly nasty fight about whether or not his mother could move into the spare room) or peeked out her broken mini-blinds to see from which direction the gunshots originated, she got increasingly glum.

Worse yet, she felt sure Salaam had a hidden motivation for buying the condo in this god-forsaken area of town, against the advice of Judy. Even early in their marriage, when the sex was good and the nauseatingly cute nicknames still dripped from their lips, he had been after her to drink and party less. He had tried everything to calm her down. When he replaced all her low-cut party dresses with elastic-waisted sweatpants, Gabrielle just rocked them with heels and cool, customized bracelets and necklaces and won the Chronicle's "Most Adventurous Fashionista" award. When he emptied out the liquor cabinet and re-filled it with Slim Fast shakes, she bought some Bailey's and made dieting fun again. Eventually, Salaam just gave up. He wondered where his sweet, demure little Gabrielle had gone--the one who blushed when he kissed her and giggled when he tried to "go too far." He tried to talk to his mother about it, but she all she had to say was "I told you so. And I warned you those Lebanese girls get really hippy in their later years!" And then she would ask when he was going to divorce that little *sharmouta* and let Mamma move to America. Most worrisome to Salaam were Ike and Darrin--he wasn't sure he liked his wife being so close to two other men, even if they did wear more rhinestones than Rufus Wainwright. The time he came home and caught them all naked in the Jacuzzi together, along with a bi-sexual bartender from the Stand Up Saloon, drinking champagne, groping each other, and loaded on Ecstasy, he forbade Ike and Darrin from ever coming into his home again. His wife in a hot tub with two supposedly gay men, and no "W" magazine in sight! Although he pretended it wasn't true, he had already heard from his driver, Josh, whom he shared with Dr. F (they both needed to cut back on their expenses, and a timeshare chauffeur seemed a perfect solution), that Gabrielle was frequently making trips from their condo down to the gay leather bars every time he was out of town. Another suspicious event occurred when he came home unexpectedly in the afternoon to discover Gabrielle and the sister of her best friend, Caroline, completely naked in the bedroom. They giggled and said they had been trying on clothes, and to PLEASE shut the door - NOW!! All of his colleagues were making fun of him for his inability to control his wife, as well as for the fact that every work event with alcohol turned into Mardi Gras, with Gabrielle flashing her (then natural) boobs and asking for jewelry. (In her defense, before her breasts had migrated south this trick had been golden--she had a stunning ruby cocktail ring and a string of black pearls from the 1999 Goldman Sachs' Holiday Ball to prove it.) Gabrielle did love Salaam, but she truly felt that Love and Sex were not the same thing--and she certainly didn't see a problem with sharing her natural assets. Beauty should never be contained—unless it was in a lacy bustier and a pair of sexy garters!

Gabrielle smiled when she remembered those days, but for the most part she felt isolated and invisible--like she was already dead, or like she might as well be. Although she had been voted "Class Flirt" in high school and could have commandeered small islands with a sway of her hips, her tactics sure weren't working now. Handsome men who would have been putty in her hands a few years ago now looked right past her and saved their lecherous smiles for the blonde waitresses offering hors d'oeuvres. And if a chubby girl in a vest and button down shirt was more appealing than Gabrielle, nothing was right in the world. If she was going to continue her rock 'n' roll lifestyle, something was going to have to be done.

The first facelift she had a few years ago by Dr. Theodore Krunkle (the hottest PS in River Stokes at that time) hadn't lasted as long as a good bag of weed. Unbeknown to her, Dr. Krunkle had a terrible reputation, and that's why his prices had been so low. A few years before performing Gabrielle's first facelift, he had been sued for showing up drunk for a rhinoplasty after drinking all day on the golf course. His shaky hands and blurred vision resulted in an accidental, irreparable shattering of the bone in the woman's nose. Fortunately for Dr. Krunkle, though he lost the golf game, he won the lawsuit, as the victim had hired an inexperienced attorney to represent her. A knee lift surgery left another patient with irreversible scars, but by then he had the legal paperwork and affirmative defenses down and avoided any serious repercussions from that one, too. So, when he accidentally cut a woman's levator muscle, leaving her unable to shut her left eyelid, he was ready to go to court again--but luckily he convinced her to settle with a lifetime of gratis chemical peels. With business faltering, Dr. Krunkle began throwing monthly cocktail parties at his office, enticing women to purchase a year's worth of Botox and Restylane at discounted prices after a few top-shelf margaritas. The fact that the fillers had been purchased on the black market in Venezuela was conveniently hidden in the fine print. The unflattering harsh lighting, meant to show every wrinkle and pore on one's face, along with the drinks and perhaps a few muscle relaxers passed from designer purse to designer purse, distracted the aging divas from reading exactly what they were signing. However, he did receive a brief spike in profits when the female robot look became all the rage--stiff faces, big lips, frozen eyes--and he sent Heidi Montag a personal "thank you" note. Unfortunately, however, the Fembot craze didn't last as long as he had hoped, and soon he was back to sticking fliers on minivans in the Whole Foods parking lot. In fact, Gabrielle got one of those fliers on her own Jaguar--but she quickly tore it up. She'd never let that old fool of a surgeon come near her with a scalpel one more time.

But soon even Gabrielle's long time masseuse, noticed that she was beginning to sag in unsightly places. "GUURRRL, your pony, Midnight, died years ago and there is NO ROOM here at the inn for those saddlebags I see. And there ain't NO push-up bra on earth that can pull those saggy puppies up. You need professional help!"

She knew that once again, Weight Snatchers and Dr. Finkelstein were calling her name...loudly. She also knew that Salaam still loved her, and he at least was still putty in her hands. He actually seemed to not really mind it when she was chubby and saggy, as it kept her safe at home with him and off the streets. Even though he couldn't afford to move them back to River Stokes, he surprised her for their anniversary with a Mediterranean cruise. They could fly into Cairo, visit his mother and brother, and then fly to Greece to start a two-week vacation among the tranquil turquoise seas of Santorini, Mykonos, and then whisk off to the cosmopolitan, ancient city of Beirut. While Gabrielle wasn't incredibly excited about visiting the original Mrs. Abdullah (that horrible, mean woman had to be longer-lived than the original Abraham from the Bible), she did like the idea of Mediterranean sand between her toes and a nice cold Ouzo in her hand. She also knew that she had to look as good as she had during her honeymoon in Monte Carlo--better, if possible.

Soon she was swiping on mascara for the first time in months, sucking in her stomach, and frantically driving to Dr. F's office for a consultation. After Dr. F finished circling all her imperfections she looked like a tattooed freak at the carnival, but she was immediately scheduled for a breast lift, tummy tuck, chin sculpt and massive laser hair removal.

Another New Nose, Another New Girl!

When Gabrielle's bruises and sutures healed and she was no longer stumbling around like a drunken sailor from all the pain medication (she was stumbling from vodka again, instead), her confidence returned. Her stomach was as taut as a twenty-year-old, and her boobs were higher than nature ever intended (but damn, did they look good). Her husband couldn't keep his hands off her, and this time around after the KPDT Christmas party, she got a choker so heavily encrusted with diamonds that she could barely hold her neck straight. Thank goodness a few of his charge cards were still operative.

The Abdullahs left for their cruise in early summer, stopping by for the obligatory visit to Salaam's mother, who, when she saw Gabrielle, wailed to Salaam that his wife had sold her conniving little soul to Satan--no self-respecting woman of Gabrielle's age had such perfect, perky cleavage. After a long three days in which Gabrielle tried to avoid the "baby" subject by alluding to a terrible (and completely made up) bicycle riding accident in her youth, Salaam and Gabrielle finally made it to the Greek Isles, where Gabrielle could almost have cried with relief. Finally--she was surrounded by beauty and luxury, just as she deserved. She only wished Judy could be here, too. They could be sunning, shopping and getting sloshed, rather than traipsing around the shoe-damaging ruins of Ephesus while Salaam read to her from his guidebook about Greek history. If she had to hear one more fact about the impressive facade of the Celsus Library or the number of scrolls it had held, she was going to drown herself in the crystal-clear water of the Mediterranean. Gabrielle had passed history in high school because the teacher had been interested in *her*, not because she was interested in it.

Gabrielle was actually quite glad when Salaam befriended a dumpy little school teacher from New Hampshire who was on the cruise with her parents so they could reconnect with their Greek heritage. From the looks of it, little Elena could have fit right in with the other Greek women in the small towns dotting the coast—she had buck teeth, a moustache, and arms that would have put a lumberjack to shame, and Gabrielle wouldn't even get started on the rest. She had slipped Dr. F's card under Elena's door one night, so maybe the poor girl could get some help when they returned to the States. Maybe the referral would lead to a free lip pump.

Soon, Gabrielle was free to sun herself on the beach and do exactly as she pleased, because Salaam had Elena and her family to drag on donkey excursions to the volcano crater and on snorkeling expeditions around the coast, completely missing the complimentary happy hours in the casino. However, she started to get a little worried when she noticed that Salaam disappeared for the entire day and didn't even return to check on her or bring her another martini. She got even more worried when she realized that, as the days went on, he was starting to look downright *happy*.

She confronted him in their cabin, waving her cocktail around wildly. "What's going on, Salaam? You haven't told me an 'interesting' fact about Greece in days, you're humming all the time, and I haven't seen you smile so much since—well, never!"

Salaam smiled, almost giddy. He looked like a leathery version of a child, he was so happy.

"I'm in love, Gabrielle. I've never felt this way before."

"In love with *me*?" Gabrielle asked, her eyes narrowing to overly smudged, mascaraed slits. (That Mediterranean humidity was hell on a make-up application.)

"In love with Elena. I asked her to marry me today on the donkey excursion—and she said yes."

"Salaam, you're married to ME!" yelled Gabrielle. "You can't just go around asking other women to marry you when you're already married. This is Crete, not Utah."

"We can get divorced when we get home. You can have everything—or what's left of it. Elena and I are going to be married in the fall, and we're going to have a family right way. She's not obsessed with her figure to the point that she isn't willing to experience life's greatest miracle."

"Because she never had a figure to begin with. And I'll bet she thinks life's greatest miracle is the return of the McRib. I hope you enjoy kissing that hairy mustache, Salaam, because you'll never be kissing me again. Well, you can kiss my ass—and even that's been waxed smoother than her face."

Within ten minutes, Gabrielle had thrown her favorite clothes into a suitcase, commandeered a donkey, and had ridden into the nearest town to catch a bus to Athens—not before hip-checking Elena into the ocean from the liner deck. However, Elena, a true Greek mermaid, floundered and sank, her bug eyes frantically huge, until a lifeguard dove in and dragged her (with great effort) to the shore.

Five days later Gabrielle had blazed a credit card trail through

Europe, all in Salaam's name, and everything she bought was two sizes too small. She was going to lose more weight and be more fabulous than ever. As soon as her spiky Jimmy Choo heels hit American soil, she had Dr. F's office on the phone and had booked a lip plumping and pit pudge removal. She had let Salaam keep her down for too long, and now it was time for a new Gabrielle to shine.

As she took the taxi home, she realized that something else was keeping her down, too—down in the ghetto, that was. The Bad Adventures condo. It had to go, and the only way was in a blaze of glory, since it certainly wouldn't be going on the real estate market.

There were only two other people in the building now (the others had either died or just given up and moved), yet Gabrielle still waited until Tuesday morning, when she knew the two old maid sisters on the first floor had put on their best sneakers and polyester pants and gone to mahjong. She also snuck into their condo and took their cat—she'd mail it to them later. Or something—she wondered briefly if you even could mail a cat, but she'd figure it out. Anyway, the fat orange tabby seemed to like her.

Gabrielle, dressed head to toe in a sexy black catsuit (like the one she'd seen in the "Batman" movies), started on the top floor with a can of gasoline and a KPDT-FM promotional cigarette lighter and left a trail of fire all the way down. Then she slipped out the back door and into her future—one she was sure would now be filled with gorgeous lovers, exotic trips, and fabulous fashion. And no nagging mother-in-law.

When she got to Dr. F's office for her consultation, cat purring happily in her Gucci tote, she was irritated and then concerned when he never showed up. He was old, after all--perhaps he had completely forgotten about their appointment, or he could have had a heart attack or something. It could be any number of other things. His personal assistant, Esther, seemed to have taken the day off in his absence, too—Gabrielle decided to make herself at home in the Judy Gibran surgery suite (named so after a hefty donation from Judy—what, giving money to a cosmetic surgical center didn't count as a charitable deduction?) and take a nap. Someone would show up eventually, and until then she could certainly use her beauty rest. Who knew arson could be so exhausting? Oh, well, she had burned TONS of calories running up and down those stairs. Her thighs would be firm, firm, firm for weeks.

Her dreams were filled with talking mustaches, turquoise water, and orange jumpsuits.

Part II

CONFESSIONS OF A PLASTIC SURGEON

Celebrity Skin

Within his bubble world of beautiful people, Dr. Finkelstein had to confess that he considered himself the most attractive of all. And when he was young, this was most certainly the case--his thick auburn hair with just a roguish hint of curl, his gleaming white teeth, and his proud, confident stride announced that he had slept with more women by the time he was twenty than most men would in their entire lives. His admiring female staff had suggested him as a contender for People magazine's "Sexiest Male Alive" in 1989, but he lost this title to Sean Connery. Even the fact that he was only 5'6" didn't get in his way--he may have been short in stature, but he was definitely LONG AND WIDE in performance. Unfortunately, he was the last to notice when his gut got a little soft, or when his hair started to thin and turned a strange, brassy orange shade a la Ronald Reagan. Through the years the twinkle in his eyes slowly dulled from charming to lecherous, and as he aged the hair in his ears and nose was growing at an alarming rate.

Knowing that plastic surgeons were the Rock Stars of the surgery world, he was still cocky. This vanity would eventually contribute to the unraveling of Dr. F's world--but of course he didn't know that when he was just starting out as a hot-shot plastic surgeon, stuffing silicone curves into everyone from Farrah Fawcett to a pill-popping president's wife to various international beauties on vacation in America. He was the only surgeon in town who could boast that his scalpel had sliced a princess from the Netherlands, a baroness from Switzerland, and the Shah of Iran's niece. He knew the secrets of nearly every River Stokes socialite (they spilled everything under anesthesia) and could be discreet. Feigning surprise upon learning of Mrs. Smith's pending divorce, he resisted adding: "Please, I knew it was coming weeks ago, when she came in for new boobs and a vaginal rejuvenation! You don't get that kind of work done to spice up a marriage. You get it done to spice up a new *life*."

Dr. Finkelstein prided himself on how far he had come from his father, Isaac's, chain of grocery stores in California's Coachella desert. Hardworking German-Jewish immigrant Isaac instilled in his son the drive to succeed and always be the very best at everything. Isaac was conservative, religious, and highly intelligent, and Barry would inherit these traits - well, everything except "conservative" and "religious." Spoiled by his doting mother, Barry could do no wrong. He had thrown a baseball through the temple window, giving elderly Rabbi Yakowitz a concussion? Youthful hijinks! He had taught his toddler niece words so bad sailors would blush and then had her yell them at Christmas carolers? Just boys being boys!

In addition to livening up his small neighborhood, Barry also enjoyed all the fine produce of the area that was shipped into his father's store and was especially fascinated by the grapefruits. The fresh, clean smell of the citrus, as well as the firm, round flesh of the honeydew melons, was intoxicating, and he could often be found fondling them in the storeroom. With his passion for produce, his parents had thought he would follow in Isaac's footsteps, so they were all pleasantly surprised when he chose to go to medical school—even if they didn't understand why he wouldn't put his intelligence to use in oncology rather than plastics.

But Dr. F was made intensely uncomfortable by mortality and the possibility of death, and striding around the cancer ward delivering bad news just wasn't something up his alley. Performing general surgery and removing gallbladders and appendixes was simply too smelly for such a distinguished man. Plastics—now there was a field full of hope and beauty and joy. No one died, and everyone woke up happy. And grateful. Perhaps at times TOO grateful. Oh, sure, Barry tried to resist, but it's hard to pass up a chance to try out your own work firsthand, up close and personal. He could justify it to himself as "research." And when he was REALLY lucky, he could get his clients to pay in cash--no hassles with the IRS that way.

When Dr. F was assigned his residency in Houston, he thought he had hit the jackpot—more warm weather, more sunny skies, and more beautiful blondes just waiting for him to buy them a drink and take him home. However, it was a petite Lebanese beauty who ended up taking *him* home—one Judy Gibran. She was struggling to get her real estate practice off the ground, and had shown him a two-bedroom bachelor pad with a view of the skyline that he immediately purchased—after he agreed to let her take him to dinner. Judy already knew that she should sleep with as many plastic surgeons as possible when she was young--because she'd seen how her gene pool aged (her own mother was sweet, but even at forty-five had been no treat for the eyes), and she knew she would need their skillful scalpels later. Using her amazing selling skills, three different costume changes, and two wiglets later, she was able to seduce him.

Their careers took off together, and Dr. Finkelstein and the woman who would become his most loyal and persistent patient, Judy Gibran, made quite the young jet-setting couple while in their early twenties. With all of his money and all of her money, they took frequent and exhilarating trips to New York City in the same way other couples went to dinner and a movie. Shopping along Park Avenue and orchestra seats at the best plays were an expected part of their dating ritual, and there wasn't a fitting room in Bergdorf's in which they hadn't had a quickie. Their fabulous good looks insured the best seats at the most popular restaurants in the city. They were front and center at the best bistros and the hottest clubs, with all the perks that came along with it. When not traveling the East Coast, they would spend time on the West Coast, playing tennis with Jack Nicholson and Anjelica Huston. Everyone thought the two would get married--and if Judy had ever dreamed of having children (which she most adamantly did not--she had seen what those little brats did to did to your waistline), the two would have made devastatingly gorgeous babies. Unfortunately, Judy was not Jewish--and the Jewish lineage flows through the mother's side. She also wasn't open to converting--all the classes and effort sounded terribly dull, not to mention that they would cut into her selling time. It would be much easier to find another handsome, wealthy lover than to learn the Hebrew alphabet, and she secretly loved bacon a little too much. So, when Dr. Finkelstein reached marrying age, his family demanded he marry a beautiful Israeli girl who had been recommended to them by a cousin. It helped that his intended, Areli, had been on the Israeli Girl's gymnastics team, so she was taut, tan, flexible, and lean.

Judy was actually fine with his decision to dump her, as she was focusing on her fast-rising, high profile real estate career. With her business and everything else beginning to burst at the seams, there was no time for a husband. Judy was a master at real estate, not just because of her selling savvy but the way she seductively licked the lead on her #2 pencil as she gazed into their eyes, and invitingly swayed her enhanced body parts as she awaited their trembling signature on the dotted line. She figured she could always make a commitment to a husband and family later, after her career had been as firmly established as her boobs. Besides, she had already gotten the best part of Dr. F--his skill on the surgeon's table and the benefits of his personal "Double Wide."

So for a while they fell out of touch, though she kept up with him through the city gossip columns, which followed the handsome, wealthy young doctor's every move with salacious glee. It was through this avid coverage of society's most sordid and extravagant excesses that Dr. Finkelstein's marriage to the beautiful young Areli became a local legend. She was the spoiled, impetuous daughter of a prosperous diamond dealer, and her parents spared no expense on the wedding of their most precious jewel. Along with each wedding invitation, the family included meals and accommodations at Tel Aviv's lush, luxurious five-star hotel, as well as around-the-clock gratis room service and spa treatments. Some guests never even made it to the wedding--they were too busy being massaged and scrubbed and exfoliated with $200 a pound Dead Sea salt blessed by a Rabbi. Ariel's wedding gown was custom made by Pierre Cardin and was trimmed in white ermine fur with a six-foot white ermine cape instead of the traditional train (PETA had a fit, and her donation of five thousand cans of Fancy Feast to a local shelter did little to quell their picketing). Her dress was also, of course, encrusted with hundreds of tiny sparkling diamonds. With her stunning, Sephardic dark looks, sexy accent, and unlimited bank account, Ariel made Princess Grace's wedding to Prince Rainier look homely, tasteless, and sadly pathetic. For three days, Israel, the land of milk and honey became a land of champagne and caviar. The timing of this elaborate three-day wedding ceremony was quite lucky, as shortly thereafter, Areli's family lost all their fortune in the 1973 Yom Kippur War. Fortunately for Areli's extended family, including her grandmother, grandfather, aunts, uncles, and countless cousins, the generous Dr. Finkelstein's frequent wire transfers kept them afloat for years to come. A nice little Hallmark thank you card sent every few years was all the thanks the good doctor ever received, and unfortunately Areli refused to stop living like a princess. So what if you could only sleep in one bedroom at a time? It would still be mortifying to have less than six, each with its own closet full of exquisite couture. And housework--Areli would put her hand to her forehead and faint if she so much as saw a broom or a dust rag. That's what maids were for.

Soon after the wedding, their first of three sons was born, assuring Areli of her position of prominence in her family and in the community. Although she was not an American Jew, and therefore was somewhat of an outsider in the Houston Jewish community, bearing sons elevated her worth to "beyond reproach." Houston's reigning Jewish matriarch, who ruled the local temple, had herself only managed six girls, and to this day it was one of her great failures.

In addition to the three sons, which Areli had in impressively quick succession, she also bore two daughters. After all these births, thank goodness she was married to a plastic surgeon. Dr. Finkelstein re-did her body from head to thigh (by then her face needed a freshening, also), chiseling her waist, sculpting her tummy, rejuvenating her vagina, and lifting her breasts. By the time he was finished with her, she looked like the young bride in her early twenties that he had married years ago. He frequently joked to his colleagues (though never to his wife's face--honesty and humor had no place in a marriage) that he had created Dr. Finkelstein's monster.

But, unfortunately, around the time of the birth of his second child, Dr. F's eyes once again began to wander. He found it hard to resist the abundance of opportunities thrust upon him-- but ultimately, the testosterone won, as it always does. It first started with one of the OR nurses. Brittany had worked for Dr. F for over five years, and they had established quite a rhythm in the operating room. Anticipating his every surgical need, Brittany could communicate with Dr. F simply by fluttering her eyelashes. Dr. F justified his first indiscretion by telling himself that statistics show that many affairs begin in the workplace--it was bound to happen eventually. And besides, the scientific evidence showed that it was totally not his fault. The camaraderie and continuity of purpose can be a bonding experience that can lead the most faithful married people astray. This bonding was exactly what happened with Dr. F and Nurse Brittany--or so he told himself. An innocent brushing of the hair from her eyes, a chance contact of the elbow against her enhanced breast (some of his best work ever), and before you know it, they were engaging in sexual acts Dr. F thought he had long forgotten. After office hours, inside the abandoned operating room--these sites were their playground. They once even engaged in oral sex while a recovering facelift patient was anesthetized on the gurney next to them. Invigorated by this renewal of his sexual powers, along with the fact that Areli didn't seem to really notice, as she was busy with the children, Dr. F began expanding his flirtations to include other nurses, receptionists, patients and just about anyone on whom he could get his manicured, well-trained hands. Even his and Areli's Polish maid, Maria, didn't escape his voracious pursuit. She was stout, uneducated and abrasive, but, boy, she could stuff a mean kielbasa. Her take-charge attitude in the family kitchen with a rolling pin had left him with memories that he would cherish forever. No matter the circumstances, Dr. F was always the best at everything he did--and he liked adding Lothario to his sexual resume.

Late Nights and Liposuction

By the late '80s and early '90s, liposuction reigned supreme as the plastic surgery of choice. Women soon discovered that paying to get that fat sucked out was a lot easier than busting their buns in cardio kickboxing, spinning, and body pump classes. Dr. F's already booming business had grown to truly impressive proportions, as did his income. At least three times a day, patients would confess to him that his plastic magic had enriched their lives, and HOW could they ever possibly repay him (wink, wink)? He was booked two years in advance and was even turning people away. He now refused to work on anyone but the most beautiful of women--there were some unfortunate feature flaws that even the most skillful surgeon's scalpel couldn't fix, and he didn't want a bunch of homely women touting his name and hurting his reputation as the high priest of beauty. Conveniently for him, these highly demanded surgeries allowed him many excuses for working late at the office and on weekends--and for dallying with every pretty young nurse on his employment roll. His business expanding, Dr. F needed more office space, and who else to call but Judy Gibran?

Judy by now had been receiving unorthodox plastic surgery treatments in Brazil, the Philippines, and Mexico--no plastic surgeon in America would touch her for fear that just one more surgery might lead to a malpractice suit. Such countries would also perform surgeries that were banned in the U.S., and Judy always did like to be the first to try any new thing, whether it was a mud mask or a new laser fat-reducing technique that might or might not result in third-degree burns.

Judy's desperate need for approval of her looks was well known in Houston even beyond the plastic surgery circle, and any clothing boutique that wanted to lure her in the door knew to cut the size tags out of the size 6's and replace them with size 2's if they wanted to be able to make enough profit to take a week's worth of vacation. And boy, did Judy buy. Every quarter she donated last season's clothes to charity and started anew, and the ladies at the Goodwill were always ecstatic to find that not only could they get Gucci for $1.99, but that they had miraculously lost two dress sizes. (Every girl's dream!)

Judy occasionally got back in touch with Dr. F to try to convince him, for old time's sake, to do a little work on her. Though he could care less about her shopping habit, as a conservative surgeon Dr. F disapproved of her desperate need for unregulated plastic surgeries. At the same time, he found himself still captivated by her charm, her wit, her wealth, and the undeniable sexual chemistry they had always shared. After she dropped by to share a chat about old times over a bottle of Belvedere (and to try to convince him to lift her boobs just two centimeters higher, "for the very last time," she promised), that old attraction (along with something else) started to rise again. Their dueling vanities were quite an aphrodisiac, and soon they soon meeting regularly at Judy's River Stokes penthouse apartment for cocktails and wild sex.

There were many clues that Judy did not consider her affair with Dr. F to be "exclusive" on her end. For example, one afternoon, after telling his wife he was delayed at the office ("Oh, that Dr. Taylor's wife is ALWAYS a couple of hours late. Her and her bridge club!") while sneaking over to Judy's apartment for a quickie, Dr. F was mortified when Judy's answering machine came on while they were in bed. Since she was tied to her antique bedpost (the actual bed in which Melanie had died in "Gone with the Wind") she was unable to reach the phone. Judy could only lie there helplessly as an African American voice left a message: "Hello, Judy, this is Curly. We met at the car wash the other night and you told me to call you real soon. I was wondering if you'd like to hook up again tonight? Call me back. You know the number. Beeeeeeeep!" Nonplussed by it all, Judy, when untied and un-gagged, defiantly told Dr. F: "Yes, it's true I slept with Curly. And you know what? He can detail my body work any time he wants."

At first Dr. F was angry--he had sent all his other paramours packing once he started things up with Judy again, and he expected fidelity on her end. However, Judy haughtily reminded him that he, in fact, had a wife with whom he occasionally still tried to sleep. Areli's lacy pink thong had fallen out of his pant leg at dinner just a few days before and the waiter had discreetly handed it back. So Judy should at least be allowed her one indiscretion--it was only fair.

This renewal of their hot sexual affair ended sadly when Dr. F discovered Judy was cheating on him with a delivery boy named

Timmy. Scheduled to view potential new office locations one afternoon, Judy called Dr. F with a strange tone in her voice, and asked him "Could we possibly reschedule our appointment for today?" As Judy was always very prompt and professional and put NOTHING above earning a sales commission, Dr. F found her request very suspicious, as well as the fact that she was already slurring her words at three in the afternoon. Oh, sure, he was used to her diet pills, cocaine, and champagne habits--it was the '80s, after all. But this time there was something unusual going on, he could just smell it (as well as a lingering odor of refried beans whenever Judy was in the room--very strange). Dr. F jumped into his brand-new silver Porsche convertible, customized license plates reading "LIPOSUC," and raced over to Judy's high rise office. Upon his arrival there, he found a Taco Tom's delivery bicycle chained to the front of the building and knew something was up--Judy would never order something so plebeian as fast food unless she had an ulterior motive in mind. Devastated, Dr. F ran up the stairs to Judy's first floor office space, where all the lights were off, even though Judy's limited edition Mercedes Maybach was there in the parking space next to the shiny ten-speed. Pressing his nose against the glass office windows, he could see the damning evidence on her lobby floor: The contents of Timmy's backpack were strewn across the room, and Judy's red-soled Christian Louboutin shoes had been abandoned on the customized brown wooden parquet. Deciding a confrontation was due, Dr. F sat down on the front steps of her office building, sadly reading his Journal of Plastic and Reconstructive Surgery (which naturally featured three articles by HIM), and waited for Timmy to leave. Two hours later (those young boys had such stamina), Judy stumbled out, her skirt twisted sideways and lettuce in her hair.

"Hi, darling," she said cheerily. "Ready to go check out offices? You can't imagine how much enthusiasm a little afternoon pick-me-up gives a girl."

Dr. F. just glared and, with his well-read head held high, limped back into his luxury automobile and drove straight to the nearest titty bar (the one where Anna Nicole Smith had once danced), and discreetly slipped into the exclusive VIP back door. Dr. Finkelstein had always loved a secret back door entrance. He couldn't say his heart was broken--she wasn't the one who had ended their affair the first time, and he knew Judy would always be Judy. But he also knew he would never find anyone else who could do what she did with her hips in bed. Oh, well. Judy is still the best real estate negotiator in town, and she's getting me a hugely discounted office lease on a primo River Stokes location. Besides, he would need her services soon when he moved his elderly mother-and father-in-law from Israel into the River Stokes area, another new luxury that he could afford--for now, at least--thanks to a recent rise in secondary surgery revisions.

However, the pressure of maintaining his lifestyle was slowly becoming too great to handle—his wife's impossible spending habits, the new cars, the fancy vacations he always had to cancel at the last minute due to pressing work schedules—each month edged his bank account closer and closer to the red and his mind closer and closer to the brink. As his hairline started to recede, so did his net worth, and as his sex appeal lost its luster, his more beautiful patients started transferring their cases to younger, more virile doctors—and Dr. F was left with no recourse: to get more business, he would have to add non-surgical procedures onto his list of services. Worryingly, there was some unknown fresh face who had just arrived in River Stokes named Dr. Krunkle, who was taking away a lot of business from him. Dr. Krunkle had come from one of those liberal states on the West Coast (Dr. F could never remember which one, and in fact referred to the competitor as "Dr. Cracker") and had made his own plastic surgery center into an all-around female Home Depot store. In addition to a good old fashioned facelift, Dr. Krunkle's office offered everything from acupuncture for menstrual cramps to varicose vein removals to oxygen facials. Dr. F knew he had to start competing on a higher level. Although he knew next to nothing about hot stone foot massages and raspberry facials, soon these items also appeared on the office menu of the ever competitive, hard working Dr. Finkelstein, politely listed beside the chin tucks and knee wrinkle removals. He began to seduce less attractive, though financially stable, chubby, menopausal housewives who were looking for a little thrill between the sheets as well as a little sprucing up. And they were always sooooooo grateful.

But still the pressure upon him kept increasing as his debt spiraled out of control and he went days between surgery patients. The initial signs that Dr. F was losing it were rather subtle at first, at least in comparison to what was to come. It all started with a simple, traditional breast lift and reduction. A referral from Gabrielle (kick back!), who had just returned from a wild music festival in Rio, had him reducing a pair of double F's down to a manageable D-cup, something he could have done in his sleep just a few years ago. But this time, he really was half asleep during the surgery, having been out all night with said patient, named Leticia, a cute little Brazilian folk singer. He had to confess that he thought the Peruvian Marching Powder had been his most intoxicating South American Adventure until he met Leticia—and she certainly was a great distraction from his shrinking bank account and his expanding gut, as well as a nice change from the flabby, overweight middle-aged WASPs from the 'burbs, who lately were the bread and butter of his practice.

Painfully greeting the new morning light, the two of them departed Leticia's suite at the Ritz and drove straight to the Finkelstein Facelifts, Facials, and More! Center. The office name change was a result of Dr. F's desperate ploy to raise revenue by approaching investors, who had demanded a fresher, more appealing business moniker. They also demanded a percentage of his profits, sending a large, suspender wearing thug in the second Tuesday of each month to recoup their return on investment.) Thankfully, Dr. F's driver, Josh, had knowingly prepared some Bloody Marys and Mimosas for the thirty minute drive to the hospital—just a little something to take the edge off. He knew how hard Dr. F had been working, both in the surgery suite and in the various bedrooms of his patients.

When Leticia awoke the next day after her surgery, she discovered Dr. F had placed one nipple facing Guatemala and the other facing Nova Scotia. This was totally unacceptable. If she had wanted a half-assed boob reduction and lift she could have gone to Mexico for a fourth the price. So WHAT if she had slipped Dr. F's Black American Express card out of his wallet when he wasn't looking to pay for the hotel suite? She was really going to make him pay for these mistakes now!

Leticia's attempt to attract international attention to her misfortune by staging protest signs as well as a feminist "Female Folk Singer Bad Surgery Blues Festival" outside the Finkelstein Facelifts and More! Surgery Center garnered few participants. Her only followers included the janitor, who thought those size Ds looked *JUST FINE*, Sarah McLachlan, and an orderly of suspicious mentality. Leticia's public relations further failed when the only TV coverage was on the Sugarland Cable TV Access channel, rather than on the national U.S. networks. As a sort of hippie chick, lawsuits were simply not her style, but she still wanted to get even with him. Flustered, defeated, and still in possession of Dr. F's AmEx card, she grabbed her acoustic guitar and headed back to Rio. Because she could no longer sing on the topless beaches she was so fond of, her popularity headed as far south as her left breast, and before long she was back to waitressing to pay the bills—so cliché.

Dr. F's ego would not allow him to confess his guilt, not even to himself. Those nipples were completely "within normal range." His inability to account for his lost AmEx card, as well as a string of mysterious charges that he didn't remember making, was just another sad drop in his diminishing financial bucket. He could contest the charges, of course, but last time he had done that had resulted in some embarrassment—he may not have remembered spending two grand at Baby Dollz Cabaret, but the pictures emailed to him later by his receptionist (along with a demand for a raise) showed that he most certainly had—primarily on a person of questionable gender named "Mai Ling."

Luckily, he told himself, a man with his talents could simply perform more and more surgeries to pay for his overhead. He might need a few little "pick me ups" to keep up with the extra volume, but so what? No one would be the wiser.

Soon, the entire town was talking about his lumpy liposuctions, his terrible tummy tucks, his fractured face lifts, and his botched butt lifts. Once again, his fortune was diminishing at an incredible pace. The few and far between consultation appointments became increasingly bizarre. A famous Italian performance artist had convinced him to implant small silicone horns beneath the skin of her forehead (she had seen it on a rock star at Lollapaloza), as well as to model her lips after a Picasso painting. Price was no object to her, as she had financial backing from a prominent Italian industrialist—never say that country wasn't devoted to art. The horn job carried Dr. H for a couple of months, at least until Areli booked another golfing trip to Scotland at $35,000 per head.

Foot Rape

The Foot Rape Trial, splashed all over the national media, was Dr. F's first brush with the law (besides the misdemeanor he got for smoking pot as a teenager). It was first picked up by just the Pasadena News, Houston Social Society Newspaper, and the local television station, KTIT-TV, but the story went viral within days—and soon everyone from queens in San Francisco to grandmothers in Hoboken were glued to the tube in disgusted fascination. Just like the O.J. trial, but without the glove and Bruno Maglis.

It all started lecherously enough. One of Houston's socialites, Dorothy "Dottie" Fainsworth, had stopped by the office for a consultation with Dr. F, begging to have her toes shortened (the latest thing—it made wearing pointy-toed stilettos so much more comfortable. In Dottie's case she had always been particularly self-conscious that her second toe was a good half-inch longer than her right. It was unsightly, and she hadn't worn open-toed shoes in years as a result; she still had nightmares about her first and only pedicure, when the small Korean girl, upon taking off Dottie's expensive leather shoe, had run sobbing from the room in fright and shrieking what had to be "Monster!" in her native language). But in every other way, Dottie was perfect. As the wife of Rice Professor Dr. Harold Fainsworth, Dottie could hold her own with anyone in a philosophical debate—her sweet smile and barbed intellect were an unbeatable combination, and if she couldn't persuade someone to share her viewpoint, she'd charm them. As chairperson of the annual Houston "Jumping Jacks for Junior League" celebrity charity event, her reputation in society fundraising was sterling. She had single-handedly raised all the money for Houston's new team-building summer camp for at-risk inner city children (which just so happened to get those little urchins off the streets AND out of polite society's sight). Her hair never frizzed and there was never, *ever* anything caught between her teeth. However, underneath her peaches and cream personality and perpetually polished appearance was true Southern steel—her background as the daughter of a wealthy rancher from Mexia meant she could castrate a bull without blinking, and as the only girl among four brothers she could deck a linebacker...which she actually did, when a football player from the now-defunct Houston Oilers had gotten a little too grabby at a charity fundraiser for cerebral palsy. The sports star, deeply mortified to have been laid out flat by such a tiny woman when even the largest of defensive players couldn't sack him, paid the city newspaper almost enough to keep a small country running for a year to squash that story.)

There was no doubt Dottie was a firecracker, and that was a large part of her appeal. Dr. Finkelstein had always had secret fantasies about the taut, muscular, cowgirl thighs that must be bursting to get out of those sweet, tight black slacks—she was so different from flighty, pampered Areli and the hard-as-nails Judy. But at social events, he could never get Dottie away from her always attentive husband—and frankly, Dr. F didn't seem like a bull she was interested in roping. She had always been polite and welcoming to him at social functions, at least in years past when he was still a Big Contributor. So it was a dream come true for Dr. F when he actually had her alone in his office, with her dainty size six shoe resting in his lap for the toe reduction consultation. His breath caught as he gazed upon her perfect hot pink pedicure (always done by herself in the privacy of her bathroom, with all the doors locked so no one would stumble in on her during that painful time) and the high arch of her foot—even her long second toe, which had caused so many socialites to spit out their canapés in disgust at pool parties, was beautiful to him.

Once again, his troublesome Double Wide became restless, and he used his old pal as a pillow for Dottie's foot. She thought the examination was a little too intense, and tried to pull away, but Dr. F would not let go of her foot, running his fingers between her toes and adding a little foot massage action into the exam. He knew he was close—so close—to booking her for the surgery (CASH IN ADVANCE), not to mention something more instantly gratifying.

Neither was to be. Tired of being politely demure, Dottie pried her foot out of Dr. F's lap and jumped back, scooping up her Manolo as she went.

"Dottie," Dr. F said huskily, "I've wanted you for years. Let's say we work out a little deal for the toe reduction—you'll get beautiful feet and beautiful memories."

The cowgirl in Dottie quickly snapped to life, and she belted the doctor right in the kisser, knocking him backwards into a potted hibiscus. She stormed out without a repeatable word, dialing her lawyer before she reached the parking lot.

While Dottie could ruin him socially (and she did—all the best doors were definitely now shut to the Finkelsteins), she couldn't completely ruin his career. Thanks to all the attorneys and wives of attorneys Dr. F had enhanced throughout the years, he had a few shreds left of his once stellar reputation, and the trial resulted in a deferred misdemeanor, despite all the hoopla surrounding it.

Hot Legs!

Dr. F wasn't the only one in his office with problems that ran deep, however. Almost every employee he had was struggling with some deep flaw or disturbing propensity. His former sister-in-law, Esther Steinberg Finkelstein Polakoff White, who was really his right hand but had no official title, was no exception. She had legs that went for miles and was one of the most glorious women to ever walk the earth from her ankles to her hip bones—but, aside from her razor sharp intellect and street smarts, the rest of her body just didn't match those impossibly high standards. Her smooth, supple calves and taut thighs were made to be showcased in miniskirts and stilettos, and stubble never dared to show its unsightly shadow on her skin. But she had a teeny little belly pooch she couldn't get rid of, her breasts were a bit too small for her frame, and she lacked an upper lip no matter how she tried to fake it with lip liner and nude gloss. All her life, Esther had heard, "She's so tall and with just a little work, she could be a supermodel." It was infuriating, especially when she saw so many girls with dumpy little cankles but pretty faces getting everything she wanted: dates, popularity, happiness.

Esther had enjoyed a small heyday from ages fourteen to sixteen, modeling plaid button-ups and denim skirts for the junior departments of companies like J.C. Penney's and Sears. In fact, with her hand on her hip, an infuriatingly saccharine smile, and an awkward head tilt toward the camera, she was known as the inventor of the "catalogue pose." It wasn't in vogue for such low-end stores to cast ridiculously beautiful teen models, unlike Nordstrom and other, finer stores, and Esther's everyday looks fit the catalogue bill perfectly. It garnered her brief respect in high school, but not for long—at six foot one she was too tall to date anyone but the blundering high school quarterback, and he was more interested in C student peppy petite cheerleaders than he was in Esther. However, he had no problem with *pretending* to be interested in Esther. He could seduce her into writing his essays and finishing his geometry homework. Alas, she was too clumsy to pole vault, and not competitive enough to play team sports like women's basketball, so for a while there just didn't seem to be any place for her. She was quite aggressive and the women's wrestling team would have seemed like a natural fit for her--but unfortunately her biggest muscle was her brain, and after one match and approximately seventeen bruises, a cracked rib, and a pulled hamstring she gave up on student involvement.

Truth be told, even Esther herself wasn't that impressed with her own modeling gigs, so she didn't blame anyone else who wasn't. As she posed in lace-trimmed tank tops and hot pants, she fantasized that she was wearing couture and storming down a runway, the fierce lights in her electric eyes and the mesmerized crowd beyond, coveting whatever designer creation her slim body was showcasing. Only Princess Diana had possessed a more sample-perfect body shape. However, when she graduated high school in her native St. Louis and moved to New York to make it big, she couldn't even make it as a waitress. She was too focused on dreaming of something better than to concentrate on carrying trays full of day-old grilled chicken Caesar salads and soggy loaded baked potato skins. However, her long legs and years of dance rehearsal did land her a one-time seasonal spot on the Radio City Rockettes Christmas Spectacular, where she would put on a pair of antlers, paint her nose red, and kick up her heels with the fat old misogynist who played Santa Claus—and who always seemed to have one present in particular that he was eager to give her.

She made her Rockette money stretch out for months before she went back to waitressing, and during that time she tried her hardest to break into the world of modeling. Unfortunately, the closest she ever got to that career was by accidentally spilling a double Bloody Mary on Janice Dickinson during her shift at Sunday brunch. As Esther was down on her knees, wiping up the ice cubes from the floor and trying to dodge Janice's stiletto, which was bobbing impatiently around her face, one of the waiters she had never noticed before (he was a full eight inches shorter and well below her line of sight) swept in and took the tables orders for her. In return, she took him to dinner—although he was merely tit height, she fell in love (for the first time).

His name was Eli Finkelstein, and he came from a large immigrant German-Jewish family of grocers/citrus enthusiasts from California. She wasn't sure how such a pale, freckled man had ever survived in the constant sunshine of that state, but perhaps that's why he had left. The perpetual smog above New York kept the sun from burning his delicate skin now, at any rate. Eli was trying to make it as a screenwriter and had given himself one year to succeed—and if that failed, he was going to go to law school. His older brother, Barry, had already graduated from med school and was running a successful practice of his own, and it was getting hard for Eli to live up to the pressure.

Soon they were cohabitating in a filthy two-room walk-up in Harlem, she desperately trying to convince anyone to cast her in *anything* (in addition to her brief stint as a Rockette, she had one more minor success as a hosiery model at a Bergdorf's lingerie show), he scribbling away at all hours of the night. But for every dream that becomes a reality in New York, a thousand more get thrown out with the garbage—and it was no different for those two mismatched lovebirds. They wanted to be able to afford more than one hot dog a day, and maybe an apartment with a window. It was time to move to the 'burbs.

It was Eli who convinced Esther to call his brother, Barry, and ask if he needed a receptionist or personal assistant—they could live there in Houston where the overhead was far less expensive, and Esther could work while Eli could pursue his screenwriting career. Esther had immediately disliked Dr. F on the phone—he sounded like an insufferable version of Eli—but she did need a job, and without even next month's rent money in her bank account she couldn't afford to be picky. Plus, she knew Dr. F was a plastic surgeon—and if only he could make the rest of her match her beautiful legs, perhaps it wasn't too late for that runway career after all.

However, twenty years and two more marriages later, life hadn't gotten much better for Esther. In fact, it had gotten worse. Though she had been one of Dr. F's first experimental breast implant patients, and therefore had a great rack to match her great legs, she was still relegated to the background. With the glaring spotlight on the less than perfect Dr. Finkelstein, no one noticed her at all. Still, she had to smile sweetly and fume secretly as she watched her boss, Dr. F., make all the money and receive all the international accolades, attention, and publicity. She had had worked closely with him for so many years that she felt she herself could now perform the surgeries blindfolded.

The only thing in which Esther could take consolation was that she was invaluable to the office. As "The Closer," she received complimentary surgeries from Dr. F several times every few years, thanks to her persuasive deal nailing tactics. She would corner prospective Plastic Surgery Recipients in a small room, peal clothing off her augmented but still beyond amazing figure to reveal whichever body part the victims were considering having updated, and say: "THIS is how great *you* can look. Now sign here. CASH ONLY. No credit cards or checks!" (These closing tactics had cost her her second husband, Irwin, who had been too prudish to deal with anyone else seeing Esther's special enhancements, no matter how fabulous they were.) She additionally supplemented her income by selling Spanx elastic girdles and silicone nipple covers at a huge mark up to the recovering tummy tuck, lipo and breast surgery patients, buying them at wholesale prices and marking them up two hundred percent. She had learned one could sell a semi-anesthetized patient just about anything.

Despite her need for additional income supporting Eli's stagnant film writing career, Eli should have thought through the move to Houston a bit more carefully. The only films being made in Houston were pathetic, non-marketable cartoon shorts, and Eli's area of interest was Baltic seafaring--an interesting choice, since if it dropped below 70 degrees he started shivering and put on his waffle-weave long Bubbas. Forced to move to Plan B, Eli embarked on the law school plan, another huge drain on his limited energies and finances. Soon Esther and Eli were forced to part due to irreconcilable differences, as well as Esther's fear that she might act out her increasingly violent fantasies of smothering him with a pillow). Unfortunately, Esther's poor body had already birthed three babies, two girls and a boy. Dr. Finkelstein to the rescue! Despite Eli's protests, he kept Esther on his staff--she was far more useful to him than his dreamer of a brother had ever been. Blood was thicker than water, but it wasn't nearly as strong a tie as the ability to close deals and cook the books.

Luckily, only one of Esther's three children by Eli held any show biz aspirations. Her younger daughter, Wendy, was a beauty pageant toddler who enjoyed some brief notoriety by winning the "Miss Southern Sass" contest held in Slidell, Louisiana, at age three. Esther had to pull the plug on Wendy's young modeling career when she discovered that in order to *really* succeed in the toddler beauty pageant world, she would have to put darling little Wendy in padded push-up bras. Even Esther had standards. There would be plenty of time later for Wendy to have fake cleavage. Instead, she enrolled her in Girl Scouts--even though she didn't believe in encouraging refined sugar consumption, selling cookies was a more wholesome activity than strutting on stage. It was a slippery slope from baton twirling to stripper poles, as she had learned from television reality shows.

Unfortunately, Sam, Esther's son by Eli, had inherited his father's dream weaver personality. He dreamed of writing the great American novel, but refused to acknowledge that there was a limited audience for a book about the history of puppets. He and his father spent long hours working on their projects together, sure that their hard work would one day pay off in fame and fortune.

Shelly, Esther's older daughter, became a successful attorney, practicing in Vermont. As a lesbian she focused primarily on gay marriage and gender re-identification cases and won most of them. Esther was fine with Shelly's sexuality, and noted that her lesbian partnerships were more successful and longer lasting than most of Esther's relationships. Plus, Shelly's partner, Lisa, was always willing to open those kosher pickle jars that were just a little bit beyond Eli's strength. And Esther still loved to suck a pickle!

Eventually, Esther reached her breaking point with her small, shy husband, and she never felt more free than the day she left Eli. She had slowly been growing tired of him for years, but it wasn't until she discovered his internet porn habit that she really lost it. That, along with his inability to keep the fish tank clean, did her in. Even years after her divorce she shuddered in disgust when she thought of his soft, clammy hands on her body and his absolute inability to ever display backbone, and she wondered what had ever drawn her to him in the first place.

But despite her disdain for the weak little man, Esther had gotten used to having someone around the house, and soon enough she was lonely and trolling the singles circuit at Rotary Club meetings and temple mixers, where she met Houston oil baron, Irwin Weinman.

Esther's second marriage only lasted eight months. Irwin couldn't seem to remember to come home from the office, but instead chose to show off his big rig to his twenty-six-year-old assistant, Tiffany. He did make it home at least one evening, when Tiffany had pulled a hamstring during the downward dog exercise in yoga class and wasn't up to their usual calisthenics. Thus, poor Esther was impregnated yet again. After the darling ten-pound baby boy, Neal, totally wrecked the perfect body Dr. F had previously created. Esther was sick of motherhood, and so little Neal spent most of his childhood and teen years at boarding schools in Missouri, where Esther's parents could keep an eye on him. A polite, good little boy for the most part, there was some concern among the family when Neal was caught masturbating while eating a hot dog during the school's "Salute to Colin Farrell" night. They assumed therapy would straighten him out, but in fact it just got him more in touch with himself (and with his therapist). By the time he was fourteen he was the only "out" teenager at River Stokes Private Academy, menaced by the football players but quite popular among the cheerleaders--no one could French braid quite like him.

Dr. F, whose firm grip on the scalpel was already beginning to falter, had to start from scratch on Esther's re-do, thanks to baby Neal. This tummy tuck resulted in a misplaced belly button and a very strange rash on the incision line, causing Esther to have to be rushed to the hospital emergency room by ambulance. It could have been worse--she had given up bikinis a few years ago, anyway, and she wasn't going to complain and risk losing her job and her income. Even though she had married money the second time around and had gotten a healthy property award in the divorce courts, her marriage to Eli had left her with an insatiable need for more money. She never wanted to have to choose between paying the light bill and paying her personal trainer again.

Even though she was becoming suspicious of Dr.F's quickly

diminishing skills (even more so when she tried to locate her new navel), Esther was a gal who always landed on her feet. And on her back--but only when there was a ring on her finger. The cute paramedic in the ambulance, Steven White, soon became her third lawfully wedded husband. And after Finkelstein and Weinman, she was definitely going to keep this fine, mild mannered Irish Episcopalian, for his easy last name, if nothing else. You never, ever had to spell it for anyone. She also enjoyed how laid back he was about his religion--while Irwin had been strictly orthodox, meaning that Shabbat dinner was required every Friday and that she had to hide her sausages in the egg carton (despite the fact that Irwin was regularly hiding his salami in Tiffany), Steven was happy if she went to church with him twice a year. He loved catching her bent over the bushes during Easter egg hunts and enjoyed the lavish gifts she bestowed on him at Christmas (compliments of her special office bookkeeping skills). Dear Steven's only flaw was his rigid, dedicated three hours spent daily at the gym, and an inordinate amount of time spent staring at himself in the mirror. He, too, would find Dr. F's surgical skills invaluable when Dr. F magically transformed Steven's four-pack stomach into a six-pack, with a mere wave of the lipo wand. And Esther was a bit more proactive this time--having learned the hard way that she was freakishly fertile, she had her tubes tied well before their honeymoon trip. Four children by three husbands was just too much to handle.

While Esther finally had her personal life together, things at the office were starting to fall apart. Though she hated to admit it, she had to confess that the constant complaints from patients about botched surgeries and missed appointments were showing a sorry side of Dr. F she had not known existed. She had heard all the gossip about his affairs, his boozing and drugging, but she had tried to dismiss the rumors. The constant replenishing of the laughing gas tank was creating suspicions among the staff, and quarreling frequently broke out during surgeries about the identity of the culprit. Furthermore,

Esther had told Dr. F not to market a "Lipo at Lunchtime" initiative, which targeted working women seeking a quick, easy fix for their trouble spots, while providing them with a light blueberry/vinaigrette salad, cup of soup, and complimentary mini-muffin. This did not go well, and the resulting lawsuits were horrendous . . . and expensive. Besides, it proved to be a really bad idea to order stale mini-muffins from Taco Tom's. What were they thinking?

The clientele at Dr. F's office had taken a decided downturn. The pole dancers and B-rated actresses coming in for anal bleaching were almost more than Esther could stand. And more often than not, their checks would bounce higher than their silicone butts--meaning that the staff didn't always get paid on payday. And for the always buttoned-up Esther, that was an unforgivable sin. The new sign Dr. F had posted at the receptionist's desk, *without* Esther's prior approval, read "Walk Ins Welcome," which Esther felt may as well have read: "Street Walkers Welcome."

Things just got worse and worse. The last facelift Dr. F had performed left a prominent society matron with a permanent, strange crooked smile and bumpy silicone in her lips, forcing her to wear a belt-like device around her head. Her sister now doubled for her during personal appearances so that the shocking photos never made it to the paper--though after being referred to in society circles as "The Phantom of River Stokes" she had a little Hermes mask made so that she could at least go to the grocery store. Then there was the rhinoplasty on the poor sixteen-year-old high school honor student that resulted in an inability to breathe through her nose—she was facing a lifetime of painful, chapped lips and was suing for pain and suffering as well as a lifetime supply of medicated chapstick. Another patient's breast implant ended up near her right shoulder. Once again, Dr. F fumbled nervously his standard response that technically this was "within normal range" and that it was "redefining perky." She didn't buy it, and a week later they were served with yet another lawsuit.

Dr. F even botched two surgeries that should have been slam-dunk operations. Gabrielle, hoping to get a discount off her own next touch-up, had referred Ike and Darren, still her very best gay boyfriends, to Dr. F. They were going on a LGBT cruise departing from Rome and sailing throughout the Aegean Sea, to celebrate their first decade together. Butt implants were all the gay rage, so they signed up immediately—what better place to show off a beautiful derriere than Rome, home of Hellenic love? Esther had lured the cash out of them by stripping down in the small, confining "closing room" and showing them her Body by Finkelstein, flashing her long legs and the seductive curve of her cleavage. Although the female body made them squeamish, especially in such poor fluorescent lighting, they both had to admit Dr. F could still knock one out of the ballpark. Or so it seemed based on the now-lovely Esther, who had come a long way since high school, and was now a truly beautiful woman. Accepting yourself the way you were was totally overrated when you could just change your outward appearance instead. It was also a lot less work, albeit a lot more expensive.

As they were cruising and sunning themselves just outside the Amalfi coast, Ike noticed that Darrin's right butt implant had mysteriously slid down the right side of his upper thigh. Because they were somewhat isolated from cosmetic surgery hospitals, they decided to cover up Darrin's flaw with a nice, floral muumuu borrowed from a member of the cruise ship's drag performers, given shape and style by a studded Givenchy belt. They could address these issues with the fine Dr. Finkelstein.

Ike and Darrin made it back to the States, more or less with bottoms intact and both sporting glowing tans, and they were in no hurry to address Ike's little problem—they had to unpack, after all—until Ike's butt started leaking black ooze. All ended well, but it was only Gabrielle's pleading and threats of blackmail that kept the duo from suing Dr. F and going on another Italian cruise.

After this last near lawsuit, which could have been the most devastating of all, Esther decided to put Dr. F in virtual "lock down" in his very own office, for his own protection as well as her job security. The loyal, discreet receptionist, who had worked for Dr. F for over eighteen years and kept all the office secrets, would remain; the one nurse Dr. F had not seduced would also stay "for appearances," but all the others had to go. They would start again, from scratch, and Esther herself would personally make sure Dr. F kept his hand (and everything else) out of the cookie jar.

Trying to re-staff at such a time was a real pain in the ass, yet Esther was the one broad tough enough to do it. Positioning the doctor's practice as "in a growth mode" among the elite River Stokes community, she was able to put the best foot forward and pull together a great new staff. Thank goodness the nursing profession was so intensely busy that the nurses scarcely had time to eat lunch, much less read all the negative publicity in "The River Stokes News" surrounding Dr. F. Furthermore, it was glamorous to say you worked for a prominent plastic surgeon at a prestigious address. No longer was Dr. F's office a playground for the nurses and staff—she forbid lunches over forty-five minutes, slashed sick days, and instituted a no-tolerance policy for showing up to surgeries drunk, high, or half-dressed. Having each new staff member sign an iron-clad confidentiality agreement was also thanks to her ingenuity. Esther also took it upon herself to rid the office of Dr. F's endless bottles of Scotch stashed everywhere, the baggies of medical grade cocaine he had hidden in the folded towels in the surgery room and inside the pages of the medical books, the strictly recreational laughing gas, and the huge stack of condoms conveniently kept right next to the gauze. She purposely overlooked the smoking green, both because she truly felt it was harmless and she herself often needed a little relaxation after a long day at work--and Dr. F never complained when she helped herself to it as a little bonus for work well done.

She then made sure Dr. F was not allowed to sign any checks on his own office account. That responsibility would go to HER now. (And if she was skimming off "a little for you, a little for me," it was only fair—she had never gotten paid what she was worth, anyway.)

Esther was especially getting tired of being on a first-name basis with the darling court summons delivery man, Timmy—he was so friendly, in fact, that the office had gotten him a nice fruit bouquet for Christmas last year. Esther was determined to single-handedly turn this office around and get a grip on Dr. F's out of control expenses— she knew that if she lost her job here, she'd never have the same amount of power anywhere else—and if she couldn't be a model, a Rockette, or a plastic surgeon, then she needed to be her most powerful best in any way she could.

When that pesky Judy Gibran began calling the office again, Esther knew it could only lead to trouble. And she was right. Fortunately, the always industrious Esther had a plan...but she wasn't the only one in the office with problems and secrets.

What a Tripp!

In the gay world, everyone knows that married men are ALWAYS bottoms. Dr. Melvin D. Tripp, Dr. F's anesthesiologist, was no exception. Born into an era where everyone was expected to enter into a heterosexual marriage and produce children, Dr. T meekly played along. Married to his high school sweetheart, Amber, who was also the former Miss Wichita Falls (or as it was more commonly known in those days, "Whiskey-Taw Falls"), Dr. Tripp had been fighting his inner demons for years--and for the most part he had been losing. While he had never been physically unfaithful to his wife after they were married, a trip to a Church of Christ gay cure camp (disguised as a "fishing trip with his buddies") had resulted in a steamy two-year cyber affair with a mechanic (he still cherished a text of Don wearing only a crucifix and an oil filter). When Amber was off visiting her parents, and he was home alone, free to view some online porn, his eyes were never watching the sultry, curvaceous women being bent over Trans Ams and across beds—instead, his eyes lingered longingly on the hard, smooth arms of the male lead, and honed hungrily in on their taut, flexing, round buttocks.

For years, Dr. T consoled himself with the fact that even though he couldn't indulge in all the hedonistic love fantasies he imagined, at least his career was going well. But even that was going South. As Dr. Finkelstein's long-time anesthesiologist, Dr. Tripp had been through the good, the bad, and the ugly in plastic surgery. He and Dr. F had met at a young professionals mixer right out of college, and they had gone through medical school, the Boards, and their residencies together. Between them, they had an unstoppable combination of charisma, looks and charm, even if the muscle-shirted young men at the country club wondered why Dr. Tripp was hitting on the leggy blondes instead of them. No straight man moved like that on the dance floor. Of course, Dr. Tripp never took any of the girls home—he just served as wing man to Dr. F, and besides, he wasn't interested in what they had to offer. He had a beautiful, sweet wife at home, even though he had to confess he wasn't that interested in her—as a lover, anyway. He thought she had her doubts about him, especially since they never made love with the lights on and he was always most frisky after watching a Hugh Jackman movie—but she was content to be married to her best friend, and if she wanted more passion she never said anything about it. Amber always appreciated his shrewd, insightful comments about her make-up and fashion accessories, and could count on him to insure flattering lighting during photo shoots at their frequent charity functions.

Plus, Amber was invaluable to him in a number of ways. When he was a young doctor building his professional reputation, he took pride in having a beautiful woman on his arm and to run his social events. Now that they were firmly established in the nouveau riche circles of Houston, his still-attractive wife's high profile involvement in charitable events in Houston society was always a good talking point with potential clients. They had built a fine family, lived in the best neighborhood, and were seen in all the right places. Amber and his children were happy, and he felt like he should have been, too—but the urges to put on a tank top and let his Freak Flag fly were becoming overwhelming.

The last few years had been tough in the plastic surgery world, and this had taken its toll on him as well. Having seen all of the hills and none of the valleys, Dr. Tripp had not been prepared for the uptrend in competition from non-board certified plastic surgeons, and the huge dent in his income this would produce. Due to its proximity to Mexico and Brazil, where a boob job could be had for $2,000, Houston was particularly vulnerable to discount plastic surgeries. A new chain called "Lipo Express" was popping up in strip centers all over town. Watching his income decline and his long time partner, Dr. F, descending into madness and depression, greatly affected him emotionally. They had always enjoyed working together, and had even participated in group sex during the disco years. Although Dr. Tripp felt out of place with the multiple girls (or even a single girl, for that matter), he was good-natured enough to go through the motions out of respect for his comrade. The medical-grade marijuana, cocaine, uppers, and downers fueled the participants and helped disguise Dr. T's secret longings. And as physicians, Dr. T and Dr. F had all the best drugs, right there in their big black medicine bags.

However, Amber had disapproved of his drug use, and Dr. T had instead begun to drink excessively as he moved out of his young experimental phase—and as a WASP, she had no problem with that. He first started sipping bourbon in between surgeries mainly to pass the time, as there were fewer and fewer surgeries requiring his assistance. His staff had been reduced from nine curvy nurses (despite his constant efforts to hire a strapping young male nurse to help him lift patients on and off the gurney) to a receptionist. Eventually, even the little receptionist only came in part-time, and soon he was downing a bottle of bourbon a day and doing pet anesthesia at the Katy, Texas, Vet Clinic for extra income.

However, on days he did go into the office instead of to the vet to anesthetize everything from hamsters to horses, the daily drive from his stately mansion in Memorial held an enticing attraction for Dr. Tripp. There was a gay bar called "The Hidden Sword" that had long been calling his name—he could just imagine pushing open the bright rainbow door and stepping into the dark world of mysterious, anonymous liaisons and maybe, just maybe, one day meeting his soul mate, someone with whom he could rent a summer house in the Hamptons or a penthouse condo in Palm Springs. He fantasized about this all day and night, doodling summer cottages on his patient files and trying on polo shirts at the Gap during his lunch break. One day, after assisting in one lonely little early morning nose job at the Finkelstein Facelifts and More! Center," he found himself in the mood for a quick little drink, even though it was only 10:30 in the morning. He tried to talk himself out of it, but it was too early for lunch at the River Stokes Country Club and he was tired of sitting in his office drinking alone every day, staring out the window, hoping for the phone to ring with a potential new patient. He hopped into his late model 6 series BMW convertible and found himself at the door of The Sword, which opened at 7 a.m. Nervously, he entered. It was a dark dungeon with torn, dirty bar stools, and certainly not sanitary in any way. It was nothing like he had imagined—he had pictured pink flamingos, pictures of Judy, Marilyn and Liza, and perfectly installed gold crown molding, but the reality was much seedier. And, er, stickier.

He approached the bar and ordered a double Manhattan. He downed it quickly, and was still too frightened to look around at the sleazy crowd that frequented The Sword on Thursday mornings. Two more double Manhattans later, and he found his confidence gaining.

79

The hot young bartender who had been mixing his drinks was smiling flirtatiously, and Dr. T was already enamored. He had never been close to a young man so beautiful before. The Sword always hired great looking, youthful bartenders in order to cater to all the old geezers who were the bread and butter of The Sword. This older crowd of queens was tamer and a little less into cruising, and now enjoyed sipping cocktails and sharing recipes instead of shots and bodily fluids. Recipes for bundt cakes, turkey tetrazzini, and seafood omelets were a frequent subject of conversation ("You simply sauté the shrimp no more than 7½ minutes"), as were their mothers' recent hip replacement surgeries and the latest furniture shipments from IKEA.

The bartenders knew to capitalize on their looks while young— they had seen what aging did to a girl, and they needed to make all the money they could while things were still firm and high. Many of the bartenders would leave their day shift at The Sword, go home for a little nap, do a few bumps of Peruvian Marching Powder, and then head off to their second night jobs as go-go dancers at the club next door. Their tip-driven dances involved letting customers touch the throbbing contents of their tiny, tight jockstraps for $1 (always a bargain).

As he and the bartender continued to chat, Dr. Tripp was elated to learn that "Doug" was the bartender's name. What a coincidence! The "D" in Dr. Melvin D. Tripp stood for Douglas. It had to be fate— Amber would be sad to lose his company and her Saturday night movie buddy, but she deserved better than him, he told himself; she deserves someone who didn't fantasize about Russell Brand when they made love.

After flirting with Doug for several hours (Doug had seen Dr. Tripp pull up in the fabulous BMW 6 series convertible, Doug's dream car) and downing six more Manhattans, Dr. T was absolutely, positively falling down drunk. Although it was still only four in the afternoon, Dr. Tripp agreed to slip out onto the back patio of the Sword with

"Doug" for a private little drink, just one for the road, as Doug's bartending shift had just ended. The patio faced an alley—nice and private, perfect for getting to know one another just a little (or maybe a lot) better.

They shared a joint that Doug had conveniently pulled out of his snug jean pocket. The boy had an ass on him that was speaking directly to Dr. Tripp. And loudly. And what it said was: "COME TO DADDY!!!" Doug's veined, steroid- and human growth hormone–infused biceps were something Dr. Tripp had only seen in the secret *Just Us Boys* and *Playgirl* magazines he kept hidden in a locked drawer in his home office. He recalled sadly the few times he had dared search for gay porn on the internet, nervous and fearful in case his wife walked in, but he now had hope of starring in a porno of his own. It was all he could do to keep from reaching out and stroking Doug's strong, firm, young, shaven arm.

His aging, drunken head bobbing to observe Doug's every inch of lean muscle, Dr. Tripp had little idea that the innocent marijuana cigarette was much more powerful than the stuff he had used in the '80s. Whatever inhibition he had left was soon completely gone, lost in the happy haze of a super hash high. After commenting on Doug's rippled six-pack, showing through his tight, tight silk shirt (stolen from the apartment floor of a one-night stand), Dr. T was invited to see a little more of Doug's gym workout results. Dr. T's quivering and drooling was starting to irritate Doug, so he simply cut to the chase—he wanted to get this over with and then take Dr. T's car out for a spin on the highway. While simultaneously unzipping his jeans, Doug pressed Dr. T's right shoulder, forcing him to the ground. Dizzy, aroused, and drunk as a sailor, Dr. T found himself realizing a life-long fantasy. Doug's veined, strong shaft was pressing against his thigh as Dr. T experienced his first male kiss—ecstasy. The smell of sweat and drug store Polo cologne, Doug's strong arm's crushing him, Dr. T felt like this experience was worth anything—anything.

Well, ALMOST anything. Except going to jail , which is what happened next. Suddenly, a cop, and NOT the cop from the Village People, was bending over them in an unpleasant way, pulling Doug off and yelling at Dr. T to zip his pants and put his hands over his head.

Dr. T's marijuana and alcohol muddled brain didn't quite know what to make of it all. "Wha?" he giggled. "Wha's this? Y-M-C-A!"

As he put his hands above his head to make the "A," the cop twisted Dr. T's hands behind his back and slapped on the cuffs.

"You're under arrest for indecent exposure. You have the right to remain silent. Anything you say can and will be held against you. You have the right to an attorney…"

As the cop pushed Dr. T toward the waiting squad car out front, he called over his shoulder at Doug, "I'm going to let you go this time, young man. Clean up your act and try to find a nice girl to make out with instead. Next time I won't be so lenient."

After the cop had driven away, Doug bent down and scooped up Dr. T's keys, which had fallen out of his pocket during the scuffle with the cop. Looks like Doug had some hot new wheels—this had worked out even better than he thought.

*****

Dr. Tripp posted his own bail and was released on his own recognizance, home in time for dinner. But his brush with Doug's forbidden fruit had lighted a fire in his loins that just would not die down. Soon he was frequenting gay bars all over town, unabashedly blasting Kylie Minogue in his car, and introducing Spanx For Men and pastels into his wardrobe. For the first time in his life, he felt free. He felt like his future was full of possibility, even though it might be lacking in financial stability at the moment.

He was returning from taking an extra-long lunch break (those were getting more and more frequent—in fact, sometimes they lasted all day) at Neiman Marcus, buying a La Perla negligee (special ordered in a size XXXL, luckily those sales girls were classily discreet and didn't even raise an eyebrow) when he was pulled over for speeding. (The police hadn't yet recovered his car, and he was driving his wife's pink Mary Kay convertible--after Dr. F's practice had started to fail, she had become the breadwinner through her uncanny ability to sell orange tinted foundation to almost anyone, including the neighborhood dogcatcher, Bubba, as well as Shaniqua, the choir director at the Ebenezer Baptist Church). Before Dr. T knew it, he was in cuffs again. Turns out that Doug's real name was Merton J. Peck, and he was an underage triple felon from Arkansas. Now Dr. T was being booked for statutory rape—and with his indecent exposure trial pending, it didn't look like he'd be getting off easy. Or getting off at all, at least not with men outside prison walls.

Dr. F's Final Fall

When Judy Gibran phoned Dr. F again, begging for silicone injections into her buttocks, Dr. F had just taken a big hit off the laughing gas. He was happy for a few minutes until the gas wore off, but after listening to Judy detailing how no one else in town would trust him to do their PS and he really did need her ALL CASH business and referrals in order to rebuild his now destroyed reputation and his finances . . . he broke down and agreed to do her surgery one last time. That Judy was relentless when she wanted something! He knew that he had done a poor job on Ike and Darrin's butt implants, but he had been flying high on some particularly fine white powder during that surgery and, now that he could only afford medical-grade weed, his surgeries had actually been improving. Not that any clients were around to notice, but he knew that if he could turn back the clock on Judy's high profile derriere he might lure in a few saggy society matrons and start his climb back to the top.

His only hesitation was his lack of an anesthesiologist--ever since

Dr. Tripp had been arrested, Dr. F had been knocking his patients out with a mixture of Everclear and codeine, telling them it was a "new cutting edge method," but he knew Judy wouldn't be so easily fooled. She probably knew more about plastic surgery protocol than he did at this point. But he bit the bullet and hired a temp--he couldn't risk losing his only client, especially when her payment would keep the lights on in the McMansion for another month.

The sequence of events of Judy's surgery are too sordid to reveal in complete detail here. With shaky hands (from celebrating with one of his nurses the night before, though he couldn't remember just what they were celebrating—maybe her engagement?), Dr. F barely made it through the silicone injections in her posterior. The loud, blaring rock music and the two nurses making out in the corner only added to the long list of distractions in the OR. Finally, as Judy was ready to enter recovery, a loud pop, almost like a gunshot, was heard. Had the Baptists mistaken Dr. F's surgery suite for the abortion clinic again? As Dr. F, the nurses, and the hospital attendants ran to take cover, three more explosions were heard—and then all was quiet. From beneath the gurney under which they were hiding, the staff cautiously peered toward poor Judy, finally remembering her unconscious presence. There was the evidence. Apparently, the butt injections had been an inferior, faulty material, and had burst, setting off a chain reaction among the massive silicone and plastics in Judy's body. First the butt implants, then the cheek implants, then the silicone lips, and finally her cherished breasts had all burst. Poor Judy Gibran's body was laid open like a gutted, plastic fish - one never to be enhanced again.

The next hour was a blur. Dr. F, immediately sober for the first time in years, took charge. He knew he would have to the face the consequences of what he'd done, but first he needed to do damage control—and pay his respects to his old friend and lover. Dr. F rushed from room to room, grabbing every baggie of white powder and every green herb he could find, flushing them down the men's room toilet and washing down the remains with a heavy dose of bleach. Then he re-dressed Judy in the chic Tory Burch tunic in which she had shown up for the surgery—he knew she would want to look as dignified as possible if any sneaky gossip rag paper photographers managed to snap a pic. He also knew she wouldn't mind—she loved the paparazzi, and one of her great regrets had always been that she couldn't get them to pay more attention to her. Appropriately, another of her many mottos was: "There's no such thing as bad publicity. And please spell my name correctly."

When the police and the ambulance arrived, he had sent his staff home and was sitting at his desk Googling himself and eating pretzels, leading to one shocker of a headline that read "Renowned Plastic Surgeon Allegedly Murders Loyal Patient and Has Nutritious, Low Cal Snack Afterward—All in a Day's Work."

He went meekly with the police to the squad car, which had its sirens blaring and its lights strobing, inappropriately reminding him of the hot disco clubs of his youth. It was the first time he'd been cuffed without a sexy nurse tickling him with a stethoscope, but it wouldn't be the last time. In fact, handcuffs were going to be Dr. F's newest accessory.

A few hours later, Gabrielle showed up for her appointment and waited in vain, an orange tabby purring in her lap and a lighter in her pocket.

Welcome to the Jungle

Unfortunately, Dr. F could no longer afford a high-powered attorney to defend him in the decade's most notorious homicide trial, and had to settle for a mere court-appointed attorney.

Timmy Ranger had just graduated from law school. His face had almost cleared up, and he possessed the enthusiasm only a fresh, young attorney could exude—one who hadn't yet been beaten down by conniving clients and apathetic judges. Recognizing Dr. F as Judy's former lover, he introduced himself. "Dr. F! It's me. Timmy, the delivery boy from Taco Tom's. And then I went to work for the D.A.'s office, and I used to—uh, drop by—your office all the time. After I first got my driver's license, I ran deliveries for Neiman's; your house was on my route almost every day. Your wife sure is pretty, too. I met her there once and gave her a complimentary chimichanga. Dr. F, I know you cared deeply for Judy and would never have intentionally harmed her in any way. I am going to do my gosh darn best to keep you out of prison."

It seems that little Timmy had traded in his ten-speed for a 3M series BMW years ago, thanks to setting the all time high "Taco Tom's Tacos on Time" delivery record his senior year in high school. This timeliness earned him a partial scholarship to college, a luxury his working class family could never have afforded, or even understood, for that matter. Thanks to dear Judy, who matched his scholarship money, he was able to go on to law school, where he was not only always prompt for classes, he was also a straight A student. Timmy could have had a job with any firm in the city—but he wanted to help people, not help screw them, and so he was working as a public defender. He hadn't won a case yet, but he knew it was just a matter of time until he found an innocent client.

Ultimately, though, Dr. Finkelstein's trial was a quick one. There was little room for doubt of his guilt—he had four eyewitnesses who had turned against him to wiggle out of accomplice charges, and they were willing to tell every sordid detail about his practice, from his assault on Dottie Fainsworth to his bad habit of munching Fruit Loops while operating (before she so unfortunately passed, Judy always had wondered what the odd circular-shaped lump was in her right breast). The prosecutor also dredged up every other malpractice suit that had been filed against him, painting Dr F in the worst light possible. On the same day that he was pronounced guilty as charged by a jury of his peers (two of whom he had actually re-done—how he wished he had botched it now), he lost his medical license. His life was in a shambles, and instead of cruising around the 610 Loop in his Audi R8 V10, he was cruising around the Fifth Ward, handcuffed in a white van and being steered toward seven years of imprisonment for involuntary manslaughter.

*****

Dr. Barry Finkelstein's first prison experiences were not pleasant. Riding in a nasty police car with no door handles, and which smelled of various disgusting body fluids, was no treat. The extremely unflattering mugshots caused him to flinch, and a feeling of guilt passed through his mind, as he recalled the horrid fluorescent lighting under which his PS clients had posed nude for their before and after photos. Gabrielle and Judy had begged him for better lighting, and he now regretted that he'd been too insensitive to provide it. If he ever got out of this mess, he silently vowed to provide nothing but flattering, soft pink lighting for his patients. All his remaining belongings were now placed into an 8 ½ ' x 11' folder. Indignant, yet too scared to protest, he reluctantly removed his crisp custom made suit, bought from the proceeds of Areli's wedding china. Submitting to the finger printing totally wrecked his manicure (traded for with Botox injections), and he hadn't had anyone's finger in the places where fingers were put during his initial body search since his "curious" phase in the '70s (though Dr. Tripp had quite enjoyed that part). He also suffered great embarrassment from the officer's raised eyebrow and muffled snort when he saw Dr. F's perfectly smooth, slightly misshapen balls. Laser hair removal and a ball lift in an attempt to recapture the glory of his lost youth had instead led to third degree burns and a side-scrotum profile that slightly resembled the elephant man's. It had also resulted in his longest period of fidelity to Areli since they had first been married, and he never slept with a woman again without the lights dimmed or without the assistance of some mind-altering substance that would ensure his conquest wouldn't even notice his lumpy love equipment.

That wasn't the worst of it, though. The initial holding cell was most uncomfortable--the grimy stark bars, the toilet with no seat, and the narrow bunk beds were a far cry from his master bath, 12' by 12' closet, and king-sized bed with crisp, custom linens back at the McMansion. In fact, his sheets here were a little sticky--and he didn't want to think about why. Worse yet were the other prisoners. One inmate rattled on and on, protesting his innocence, and another street bum seemed happy to be in jail in order to have a shower, some food, clean clothing, and a place to sleep. Dr. F simply *had* to have a private cell. He had an M.D.--he couldn't be sharing space with a high school dropout from Arkansas who had been arrested for marrying his own sister and a misogynistic plumber who had violently suctioned his girlfriend during a domestic dispute. Unfortunately, Pete, the lazy guard seemed to be more interested in his state-supplied bear claws and instant coffee than Dr. F's discomfort. However, the handsome Prince Charming in Dr. F re-emerged after years of dormancy, and by promising free lipo to the guard for his wife (Dr. F had seen the woman's picture on the guard's desk, and she definitely needed it--you could fill a truck bed with all the fat that was in that woman), was able to get moved to a single 6' x 8' cell. The sheets were still sticky, and the toilet was still stainless steel, but at least Dr. F could sleep without hearing another inmate's heavy snoring above him.

Dr. F had always been a man of his word, no matter what the circumstances or condition of his mental state. Aware that he had promised Pete, the security guard, complimentary lipo for his wife, Dr. F was concerned that he had no anesthesiologist. He couldn't possibly suck out that much fat out of a woman without her being unconscious. The guard wasn't in a hurry--the promise of a free surgery had made his wife so happy that she voluntarily picked up some fried chicken for dinner a couple of times *and* was nice to his mother on a regular basis--and he agreed that they had to wait for the most opportune time. He wasn't eager to lose his job, and he was pretty sure there was something about letting unlicensed doctors performing midnight surgeries that could get him fired with no severance.

Dr. F's elite, debonair demeanor was intimidating to the other prisoners, and this worked in his favor in interactions with the other inmates. At first, they were none too welcoming to this small, ginger man in their midst. How did a smart, rich, handsome man like that end up here with us? they thought. The gang members were so confused, trying to figure him out, and so for the most part they left him alone. Usually, the lowest on the prison hierarchy and most likely to be molested were the child sex crime offenders, who were assured a most uncomfortable stay behind bars. Fortunately for Dr. F, the violent gang members did not read newspapers, and in any case certainly would have been confused by the Foot Rape Trial. By offering complimentary tattoo removals and teaching them how to play pinochle, Dr. F gained supreme status among the prisoners. Besides, there were younger, better looking guys to fondle in the shower. Soon the entire prison staff as well as the inmates regarded Dr. F as King. The guards provided him with a lovely full length mirror so he could admire the results of his prison gym workouts. His food deliveries from the Z Hotel, long ago arranged by Timmy, were nutritious and low fat. If he was going to be incarcerated, the least he could do was to look good. His long dormant musical aptitude rose, reminding him of his great passion for rock and Memphis soul music, when little - what was her name? Oh, yes! *Gabrielle* could get him front row tickets and a parking pass, and he proudly led the prisoners in Sunday Morning Sermons in great Christian spiritual hymns such as "Walk to Jerusalem" and "Amazing Grace." The circle prayers and group hugs were at first uncomfortable, but eventually served to bond the prisoners.

Luck smiled on Dr. F in more ways than one, however. During a particularly nasty influenza breakout, Dr. F, who by now was highly regarded as a model prisoner with excessive privileges (he had started tutoring the warden's daughter for her MCAT, and she had passed with flying colors), stepped up to volunteer to help out in the infirmary. Not only might he get some more privileges out of it, but there were usually some really cute nurses he could hit on there! The last three times he had had food poisoning from Breakfast Burrito Wednesdays he had taken comfort in the arms of a particularly curvaceous young thing named Sally, and he hoped she had already forgotten the less-than-attractive sight of him heaving sweatily into the toilet. But all thoughts of playing doctor with a cute nurse (or any nurse- she could be built like a linebacker for all he cared. It had been tooooo long!) vanished when who should he run into but his former soul mate, Dr. Melvin D. Tripp. Dr. Tripp was assisting in the infirmary as well, and had been bused in from a neighboring prison as a favor between the wardens. Soon they were a team again and completely in sync, dispensing medicine and supplies to the poor, sick prisoners. What a relief to have someone else in this lousy prison who thrived on reciting golf scores. The warden was so pleased with their work that he pulled some strings and had Dr. T permanently transferred--though he adamantly refused Dr. T's offer to sew sequin spangles on his jumpsuit. He did back down, however, and allow Dr. T to pad the shoulders a bit and add a chic cloth sash, the better to accentuate his trim waist.

Luckily, their surgery on the guard's wife was a success. In the dead of night, after the medical staff had all gone home, the guard sneaked Dr. F and Dr. T into the infirmary, where he had already laid out all the tools they had requested (Timmy had kindly dropped them off with the guard earlier that day--he was so glad to see that Dr. F was already becoming rehabilitated!). Three hours and six gallon buckets of fat later, the guard's wife had been transformed from a tubby terror into a svelte sex kitten.

The successful surgery on the security guard's wife renewed Dr. F's self-confidence and energized Dr. T's suffering self-esteem. Soon they were operating on the wives of other male security guards, as well as the female guards, specializing in tattoo removal, anal bleaching, and vaginal rejuvenation. Timmy, who had always known that Dr. F was a really good guy deep down inside, had befriended the prison's purchasing agents and arranged for periodic delivery of the vast array of products and equipment necessary for Dr. F's surgeries. Oh, sure, Timmy had to provide legal services to the bursar's teenage son, who was a crystal meth addict, but anything to help Dr. F. As far as Dr. F - Why, this was the best work he had done in years! He truly was the Plastics Magic Maker of old once again. He had even lost some weight and (or at least he liked to think it) and gained back some of that receding hairline due to hours with nothing to do but rub Rogaine into his scalp. Having been forced to give up liquor and drugs by what he thought were the overly harsh prison rules had also improved his health--he almost felt like a young man again!

Dr. F's special skills did not go unnoticed by the prison's female psychologist, Dr. Holly S. White. A very attractive girl, she had an unfortunate chin wattle, which Dr. F sucked out. He also threw in a nice new set of cheek implants, as well as removing a couple of unsightly moles. With these improvements, and a complete wardrobe and cosmetics makeover from Dr. T, who was studying for his cosmetology license in his spare time, she was finally getting asked out on dates by men who didn't still live at home with their mothers. These fine gestures and her boundless gratitude for their life-changing services assured that Holly would recommend to the parole board an early release from prison for Dr. F. That anesthesiologist's advice had changed her life as well (she couldn't believe now that she had ever worn open-toed shoes with hose!), so she rubber-stamped a release recommendation for him. Soon the boys would be out of prison. Unfortunately, they had no homes, no cars, and no wives. What to do?

Dr. F had to confess that he had known in his heart that this glorious day would come sooner than everyone else expected. He had been listening to motivational audio tapes and trying to awaken the giant within while channeling the power of positive thinking. And as Dr. T was practicing his makeover skills on the prison guards' wives, Dr. F had been writing his memoirs titled "Plastic Surgery: CONFIDENTIAL."

His expose on celebrities and debutantes -WHO had a third nipple removed? WHAT famous pair of breasts were actually silicone? WHO is a good candidate for rhinoplasty? - gave his book instant appeal in the tabloid-saturated media market, and soon several publishers were in a bidding war over his expose. He took his time choosing, knowing that his interviews behind prison bars were merely fodder for the publicity storm. Besides, he really had nothing else to do there at the prison, and he enjoyed this unexpected renewal of his long dormant Star Power. When he finally signed a publishing contract, it headlined every entertainment gossip show--and when the book was released shortly thereafter, the prison even held a special book signing in his honor. Dottie Fainsworth, media whore that she was, quickly switched sides and told the press that although he had nearly screwed up her toes, Dr. F had once given her the best facial of her life. Secretly, she was hoping Dr. F's book would lead to a reality TV show based in Houston, with her in a lead role, showcasing her favorite charities and her automobiles, while she modeled all her finest custom jewelry, couture outfits and gel nails. Suddenly everyone wanted to jump on the Finkelstein Band Wagon for a free ride and a little publicity. Even the governor came, smiling and giving sound bites about the successful rehabilitation of hardened criminals.

With a huge advance from the publisher, as well as all the money from the book pouring in, Dr. F was quickly replenishing his lost fortune. Demanding "Entertainment Now As Before!" pay an unheard of seven figure sum for an exclusive, behind the scenes scoop, Dr. F proved just how persuasive and charming he could be. His time at the prison gym insured that he was more than camera ready. Certainly, he would loan a few bucks to his destitute comrade, Dr. Tripp (who was now paying exorbitant amounts of alimony to his dear ex-wife, Amber). Besides, with virtually no overhead, and no drug habit, Dr F. was rolling in dough! They would be back on the golf course in no time.

Of course, Dr. F did have some regrets that he could no longer practice surgery (legally, at least). Without his medical license, he wasn't sure what he would do when he was actually released, especially since he had accidentally killed his most loyal and profitable client. If only Judy had had a sister who also desired such extensive reconstruction of every part of her body. But oh well. Dr. F was sure he would land on his feet--he always had before.

Part III

Confessions of a Plastic Surgeon's Wife

Charming Woman, Charmed Life

Ah! The privileged and blessed life of the wife of a plastic surgeon in Houston! Juggling your schedule to fit in the personal trainer who comes to the house three days a week and supervising the personal chef, hired away from a Michelin three-star restaurant in Beverly Hills, who specializes in low-fat, low-carb menus. The constant maintenance of the lush grounds and pool at the Finkelstein estate, strategically located on the very best street in River Stokes, the daily interactions with hairdressers, make-up artists, masseuses, and stylists. And still making time to hang on your husband's arm at every charity event and society party—but Areli had to confess that living this life was simply exhausting. Keeping up with it all meant she never had a true moment to herself or a second to rest. Seeing the same old wealthy Houston Power Brokers over and over again was so tiresome. Furthermore, all those insultingly ridiculous rubber chicken lunches and dinners at the River Stokes Country Club with abhorrent oil men wearing '80s shelf hair-dos and their starved, young, bleached blond trophy wives with cheap, tacky boob jobs was wearing on Areli. Oh, well. Limp lettuce and soggy creme brulee were easy enough to avoid—she could whip up a previous obligation at the drop of a hat ("Well, I absolutely MUST attend Sara's play--she's only a tree, but my mother forgot one of my performances and I STILL have not forgiven her. You simply don't know what parental neglect can do to a young psyche"). So forget about the endlessly dull golf games where she could barely work in a crisp little vodka/soda. Golf?! She had never been a girl to wear plaid—the Houston Opera was much more her style. There she could dress up in her most flattering gowns and highest spikes and take command of the room as the most photographed woman there, with the most fabulous legs and regal posture, elbowing the sad little wannabes out of the shots. Plus, she found something particularly poignant in all those operatic forsaken wives and lovers wailing their hearts out in song—she identified with them more than she liked to admit.

As the years went by, Dr. F had become more of the arm piece for Areli, rather than the other way around—though he was now balding and paunchy, his wealth and obvious skill with a scalpel kept him handsome and desirable in other women's eyes—and if Areli knew he was too easily attainable by her fellow socialites, all hungry for an afternoon affair, she never let on. To her Dr. F was still the slim, handsome young man she had married, the one who brought her flowers and surprised her on her birthday with a private string quartet to serenade them during a picnic lunch in Hermann Park.

And despite his indiscretions, Dr. F was still noticeably fond of her when they were together—his hand in the small of her back guiding her across rooms, quick to open doors, dropping frequent kisses on her forehead. It was this very sweet solicitude, in fact, that made the other wives so eager to get their own claws into him—their own husbands had long since stopped being so attentive. They didn't realize that Dr. F's affectionate gestures at charity events were the attentions you would bestow on a beloved pet, and that the Finkelsteins hadn't been close as a husband and wife should be for years. Areli loved him and all the attention being a surgeon's wife brought to her, as well as the perks of being married to a wealthy man, and so she was a little more willing to overlook the shallowness of their marital bond than she perhaps should have been.

Dr. F was still drawn to his wife, of course—he couldn't help it. Areli's charisma was undeniable, and a glowing light seemed to exude from her very soul. She charmed almost everyone with whom she came into contact--because, despite her slightly spoiled demeanor, she was genuinely a kind woman. She liked to make people happy, and she liked to be loved. She couldn't help it that she expected the very best, or that she frequently found herself helplessly baffled in everyday situations. She had been born with a platinum spoon in her mouth and hadn't even started dressing herself til age sixteen, much less gone to the grocery store alone and encountered such a frightening array of yogurt brands.

Early in their marriage, before kids but after the blissful honeymoon phase had started its sad, slow fade, she had come home with an entire trunk full of whole wheat bread, much to Dr. F's dismay. As he saw her carrying in bag after bag, he stopped her in the driveway.

"Areli! What's going on? You went out for a carton of eggs, not to buy enough bread to host a dinner party for every pigeon in the city."

Areli's eyes welled up with tears—she hated when Dr. F criticized her, and it seemed like he did it more and more lately. She had thought when they got married that they would be inseparable, that couple who finished each other's sentences and never spent a moment out of each other's sight. The only time she felt close to him now was when he was planning her next surgery—he was always very tender and loving then, as he circled her spots of cellulite with his purple surgery marker.

"I got so confused!" she snapped defensively. "You fired our house manager and she didn't leave me any instructions--and there was an entire *aisle* of bread in that store. Sliced, unsliced, gluten-free, honey-top, organic--it was overwhelming. I just bought it all, and then my cart was so full that I couldn't even get to any of the other things on my list. I'll have to go back tomorrow, I suppose, but I'm so exhausted from today that I can't imagine it. I might go to the spa instead."

Dr. F hired her a new house manager the next day—he figured that was cheaper than spending hundreds of dollars a week on every brand of pate, cheese, and dryer sheets under the sun, as well as the inevitable $1,000 spa day that would follow. Of course, this only reinforced Areli's "If you could hire someone for something, why do it yourself?" motto. She believed in that creed simply and fully, and as someone who had only witnessed poverty from the window of her limo while driving through the 5th Ward on the way to the Jones Theatre downtown, her worldview had never been shaken.

This motto didn't extend to her children, however, and Areli prided herself on being a devoted and loving mother. It was the only area of life where she felt truly confident, happy, and competent. Of course, her fellow socialites didn't see her dedication to her children in quite the same light, and they started gossiping furiously whenever she was out of earshot.

"She was wearing a *Bjorn* strapped over her Pucci tunic the other day. Completely clashed with that divine pattern. She obviously doesn't respect the Pucci. It's a *crime*. I literally shuddered."

"And did you see her playing in the sand with her children the other day? *Barefoot*? I can't tell you how much I paid Su Win for this last pedicure--the woman's charges are out of control. Dr. F just must be made of money for her not to even consider the state of her feet."

"She picks the kids up from school, too—herself. Every day. I can't imagine making the time to do that—or sitting in that dreadful pick-up line. She got dinged there the other day by a Kia. A *Kia*! I don't know how those parents can embarrass their children by picking them up in that, but it takes all kinds, I suppose. I would never let my mother pick me up from high school in anything less than a Benz. She came in the Cadillac one day and I refused to get in the car. I mean, *really*? What kind of person drives an American car? My boyfriend almost broke up with me over it—I can't even tell you what I had to do to keep him."

The gossip got cattier as the years went on, but Areli always thought the best of everyone and assumed they were complimenting her selfless attempts at motherhood, not criticizing her. And while she had sacrificed her trim figure and petite vaginal opening to bear Dr. F's five children (and she was eternally grateful that they had inherited her own dark Sephardic looks rather than his Ashkenazi complexion), she would genuinely say that motherhood was worth it. She cheered at soccer games, chaperoned school field trips, and hosted huge, elaborate slumber and birthday parties. Nothing but top of the line bakeries for the birthday cakes, cookies and cupcakes! She was everyone's favorite mother—except, of course, for the other mothers, who were appalled at how bad Areli's own maternal devotion made them look. However, they took comfort in the fact that Areli's progeny, despite her commitment to fulfilling their every need, were not exactly the cream of the crop.

Unfortunately, while Areli's children had inherited her beautiful, creamy complexion and striking amber eyes, they had also inherited their father's laissez-faire disposition—minus his drive for wealth. They were gorgeous, spoiled, lazy, and unambitious--each one of them. But Areli still thought them all darling little angels, and she was genuinely sad when they left the nest. Though they dutifully called home once a week, it was usually to ask for money. Her youngest went to Rice University so she could still visit him, which she did with great enthusiasm. She frequently showed up at his dorm room with fresh brownies laced with weed, as he liked (she so tried to be cool and he would never know what a hardship it was to control herself and not lick the beater *even one time.* She knew that giving that lick would lead to a carb orgy that packed ten pounds on her hips). But he was usually too hungover from the heavy metal concerts from the night before to go to the art museums or even Sunday brunch with her. She missed the days when her children had all been little and needed her, even though it had been almost impossible to fit in all of her other social and personal obligations on top of motherhood.

*****

As Areli began to age, along with the mounting financial pressures at home from Dr. F's failing plastic surgery practice and her personal ambition to be the Best Mom Possible, the constant dictate to always look Her Very Best Always (after all, she was a 24/7 walking spokesperson for Dr. F's surgery magic) was wearing on her-- especially since she was competing with the new wave of trophy wives who had entered their social circle. About every four and a half years a fresh crop of perky, fit, fluff-brained young women married into River Stokes society, looking pityingly at those women who had managed to maintain their husbands—it must be *so hard* to be over thirty! But those girls always came and went—usually looking more like leather handbags than not from the excessive tanning at their lavish mansion pools. Areli prided herself on her light olive skin—it hadn't seen the sun untouched by SPF since she was a toddler, her mother had seen to that—and while she might not have the flat stomach of a twenty-year-old, at least she didn't yet need Botox or those frightful chemical peels that kept you locked up in the house for at least a week afterward.

But even greater than the social pressure to age gracefully (or rather to stop time in its vicious tracks) was the pressure to graciously "give back"—which was required of society wives. Hostessing scores of Houston's major charity events was thus a huge part of her very serious role as the wife of Houston's most revered plastic surgeon. Since Dottie Fainsworth had blacklisted the Finkelsteins, Areli's last fundraiser hadn't netted enough to pay for a Brazilian bikini wax. It

102

was just all too much to bear. Areli remembered with discomfort the last time she had run into Dottie at spin class—though Dottie had been flawlessly polite, Areli could feel Dottie's simmering anger filling the room; the woman was a master of haughty disdain, able to mask it over with a veneer of Southern propriety--but it had never before been directed at Areli. The last time Dottie had targeted a fellow socialite, it had been for wearing the same Herve Leger dress as she at an event— after a vicious treatment to Dottie's Southern charm ("Oh honey! You do have the curves to fill out that dress—pity they're all about four inches too low. Let me give you my nutritionist's number..."), the woman had left in tears. Dottie's rage was a powerful thing—and Areli wasn't entirely sure there wasn't some black magic involved in punishing those who wronged her.

Areli had left in the middle of the spin session, claiming a headache, but really she just couldn't bear the pressure of being in the same room with Dottie. What did a woman with a freakish chimp toe have that she didn't? Why on earth had Dr. F been so enamored with Dottie? And Dottie had turned on Areli so quickly—what had happened to sisterly solidarity? She was hurting, too. They could have taken the awkward situation as an opportunity to commiserate on the hardships of being a society wife, maybe sharing a bottle of red wine while becoming best friends, just like in the movies—but Areli hadn't ever found a friend like that, and it didn't look likely to happen now, either—the only women who would talk to her now were her maids, and even they weren't all that polite. Areli was also mourning the final crumbling of the fairytale marriage she had built in her head—until Dottie had confronted her about Dr. F's philandering, Areli had always been able just to look the other way and ignore the situation. Now, however, she had to face each morning with the knowledge that her husband was unfaithful. And if she had to admit to Dottie, then she had to think back to all the years before and start listing the suspicious incidents in her head—and she couldn't bear to do that.

Despite their financial troubles, though, Areli had found a way to relieve the stress and the loneliness, Texas Style—more shopping. Her house was empty without her beloved children, and so she decided to fill it with things—clothes, paintings, enormous flowerpots—it didn't matter. It was therapy, and one of Areli's earliest memories involved her mother taking her to the furniture market after a particularly venomous fight and re-decorating the house (toward the end of her parents' marriage, their house went through more decorative schemes than a Dillard's window). Even though she knew better, Areli soon found herself paying full retail prices for her clothing. In fact, her spending was so out of control, Dr. F referred to her as "Retail Plus." Esther's gay son, Neal, now living in Manhattan, was working as a buyer for Barneys and could have given Areli fabulous merchandise at huge markdowns—in fact, he could have sent her items from the sample lines for free. But even his generous and frequent gifts, arriving in gorgeously wrapped red and black boxes, weren't enough to fill the void in her heart. As Dr. F left the house at the crack of dawn weekdays to perform his surgeries (or, more often now, to sit glumly at his desk and wait for lunch), Areli found herself breakfasting alone daily on a double espresso and then running over to the Gallamaria to shop, shop, shop. The daily deliveries to her home had definitely slowed down, since half of Dr. F's credit cards mysteriously began to be refused. However, at the Gallamaria, all the shop clerks recognized her as a loyal customer, and furthermore trusted her from her numerous society photographs—someone who cared so much about adult orphans and the preservation of rare Thailand guppies must be trustworthy—and somehow the charge cards were run through. If they didn't, then Areli just opened a store card. The economic downturn had hurt retail sales as savagely as it had hit plastic surgery, but stores were so eager for the business they were sloppy in their background checks. Additionally, the poor starving sales clerks worked on commission, and they were happy to skip a few steps in the credit card processing so as to be able to collect their paychecks before the store's accounting department caught up with them. Hopefully, they would be onto their next job (in acting or modeling, of course) before the stores even figured out the accounting errors.

At last, all the credit card juggling was gaining on Areli, and she began charging her little goodies to other people's accounts. She would simply say that she had lost her credit card, and would you PLEASE just charge it to Esther White, her husband's long-time office manager? She kept a detailed list of all her purchases and planned, with full faith, to pay Esther back. However, her lack of real-world skills was finally catching up to this woman who had until now lived a sheltered and charmed life. Her strict wardrobe standards still intact, she would return a pair of sixteen dollar tights if the color was "off season," but when she had a Fashion Blackout and purchased a green hobo Gucci purse that went out of style within thirty days, she simply gave it to Goodwill for a tax write-off rather than returning it for store credit (a great tip from Judy Gibran. The woman was terrible and a home wrecker, but she gave great financial advice). Areli had no concept of money, because that had never been required of an Israeli princess such as herself.

But despite her helplessness with day-to-day life, Areli was too intelligent to ignore what was going on around her, including her diminishing status as the Premiere Plastic Surgeon's Wife. As a result of Dr. F's constant drinking, drugging, and womanizing, and while she smiled and put on a "loyal wife" front about it she was getting mad as hell inside. She remembered when she had been a young girl of twenty-two, just out of college in Israel and looking forward to fulfilling her dream of becoming a gym teacher. No, it wasn't glamorous and it paid less than her monthly allowance, but she loved kids (that's why she ended up having five), and at that time she had her family's fortune to fall back on. Plus, she looked damn amazing in spandex and a headband. But then she had been introduced to Dr.

F by her cousin, and she had immediately been smitten. Even though she wished he was a bit taller, she was taken by his charm and the playful twinkle in his eye. He was dashing and brilliant and wanted her—Areli!—and so she had given up her sneakers and her virginity to the charismatic doctor. If her parents had known that she'd slept with Dr. F before the wedding, they would have been appalled— they had guarded their daughter's flower so closely that she hadn't ever even been allowed to attend an all-girls' sleepover, for fear of illicit experimentation. But once she and Dr. F were engaged they had loosened up their rules a bit, and by the time Areli was walking down the aisle in white she was already carrying Dr. F's first son (and convincingly blaming her extra five pounds on all the fine caviar her mother had forced her to sample while they planned the menu).

Although she loved her family with all her heart, Areli had to confess that she was actually glad to leave them behind to move to the States, even if it meant shedding the elegant Hassar surname for the slightly gauche Finkelstein moniker. Every family has a few crazy relatives, but it seemed to the sensible, conservative Areli that her family tree was loaded with nuts. In fact, it was a veritable pistachio tree. Her ancient and leathery grandmother, Elisheva, bore a strange attachment to her oldest son, and when introducing him to American travelers would announce to the world: "He's not my son, he's my *lover*! Just look at him! He is so beautiful! I carried him inside me for nine months!" More disturbingly, her handsome son (for he was truly the Jewish incarnation of a Greek God—perhaps Zeus) just smiled benignly at her comments. Although crazy seemed to be a family trait, Areli seriously doubted that true incest was going on behind closed doors and disregarded the remarks as overly affectionate at worst and a mangling of the English language at best.

"Life's short- Party hard" and "Everybody Middle Eastern Unisex!" seemed to be the Hassar family philosophy (though not in her branch of the family—if her parents could have forbidden her to leave

106

the house entirely they would have). Her female cousins seemed to do nothing all day but go to various beauty salons around town: one shop for hair extensions, one shop for make up application, another shop for full body waxing, and two more for mani-pedis. After hours on end of getting all dolled up, the girls would furiously drive around Tel Aviv, hunting for men. Her second cousin, Devorah, was a particularly aggressive driver in bumper to bumper traffic. As they tooled around in Devorah's Mercedes, Devorah would practically bang her bumper into the rear of any good-looking male candidates' cars—a small fender bender was a sure-fire way to get their attention *and* their phone number. Upon spotting one prospective dark-haired hottie, Devorah almost took out two pedestrians and a moped until she could pull up next to him, batting her false eyelashes and shaking her hair extensions in his direction. Alas, after this wild chase through rush hour traffic, Devorah found that upon closer inspection, the hottie turned out to be less than attractive. "Look at him. He's all hairy. He looks just like a monkey. Maybe I just show him this!" she said with disappointment as she pulled her blouse down over her shoulder. Better-looking (and thus more fortunate) candidates got to see much more than just a bare shoulder, frequently resulting in traffic accidents that Devorah zipped away from while laughing. Areli spent these afternoons clutching her seat in fear and was usually too nervous to eat for days afterward. But her parents thought that Devorah was such a nice, temple-going girl that she couldn't be anything but a good influence on their own daughter. Little did they know that Areli was taking part in a ride-around-town peep show, starring Devorah's left and right knockers (depending on which side of the road the man she was pursuing was driving on—and she was not averse to slamming the car in reverse for a backward pursuit, either).

Devorah further showed her lack of refinement when Areli was visiting the Israel Museum by harassing Areli with phone calls saying: "Areli, why you want be with dead people? Let's go Budda Bar. Let's go Sky Bar." Meekly, Areli protested that she was enjoying all the ancient artifacts, and they could catch a drink sometime later, perhaps *after* lunch?

For the most part, the male cousins were good-looking and as vain as the women. It seemed all they did was gamble and stare at themselves in the mirror. They were notorious for sharing pictures of their ripped stomachs and penises on male-only internet web sites, competing for the most page views. "Look!" boasted Aaron with pride. "Seven hundred people have downloaded my manhood as their wallpaper. Our cousin, Efron, only has *three hundred* downloads. I always told him size matters. That is why his beautiful girlfriend left him for that tall Swedish man she met in Geneva." Poor Areli would watch reruns of American TV shows such as *The Waltons* and long for a normal, well-adjusted family that was full of love--though she didn't want to live in poverty in the mountains, of course. Maybe Paris or New York, somewhere with shopping and culture and class, but where she could still teach dodgeball and flag football to children—that sounded ideal.

The night before her wedding, another unfortunate incident with her relatives occurred. While riding in the back of her Uncle Benjamin's Mercedes, along with her Aunt Rachel and other members of the wedding party, they were pulled over for speeding by the police. Areli knew this would not be good. Areli's wedding flashed before her eyes, as she envisioned them all spending the night in jail and her expensive buffet slowly growing cold, untouched. Although deep down he was a most kind and generous man, Uncle Ben had a hot temper and a filthy mouth. He was used to doing things only one way: HIS way. Ben was enormously wealthy and more or less paid people to be his friends. Envisioning himself as above everyone else, there was no way he would tolerate a lowly police officer's reprimand. Using Arabic swear words (as there are no swear words in the Hebrew language), Ben told the police officer to "Tilhous teezi!" which, of course, translates literally to "lick my asshole." Just as the officer began the arrest procedure, Ben pulled a rabbit out of his hat by faking a heart attack. Flustered, the police officer merely issued a warning, and the wedding party sped off to the "hospital." The next day at the reception, Uncle Ben managed to work the story into his toast—causing everyone in the family to crack up with laughter and causing Areli to bury her head in her hands: the words "lick my asshole" were now on her wedding video forever.

But their glamorous honeymoon erased all bad wedding day memories of a less-than-refined family—luxurious breakfasts in bed and leisurely boat trips down the Seine, all while being the complete focus of Dr. F's adoration, made for the happiest two weeks of Areli's life to date. At first, their marriage had been wonderful—Dr. F was attentive and gave Areli everything she wanted and more. They immediately became society's it-couple, invited to every party and honored guests at charity events. But in time Areli couldn't help it when Dr. F's eyes begin to stray—first to the sturdy Polish maid (she was ugly and mean, but she could stuff a mean kielbasa). And then to his nurses and then, time and time again, to that horrible, crass Judy Gibran. Areli, who still loved Dr. F, just pretended the affairs weren't happening, hoping her husband would come back to her exclusively, but she slowly grew more and more fed up despite the lies she told herself. Soon she was indulging in passive-aggressive retributions like picking out the middle initials on his custom made shirts and deliberately dinging his car door with hers each time she parked. It may have been childish, and she would never admit to doing it, but it sure felt good.

Finally, after the Dottie episode, Areli had hit a wall. The chef had stormed out, raging about not being paid in over two months, meaning that Areli was relegated to either ordering in salty Chinese every night, which caused her to retain water, or trying to cook--and her youngest child, who was occasionally guilted into visiting home, was not impressed by her Vienna sausage surprise. Furthermore, the last time Areli went to the country club the doorman had coldly escorted her out. Their dues were way past due, and their membership had been passed on to her nouveau riche neighbors, who had made their fortune off strikingly realistic blow-up dolls, of all things. And as the last straw, things kept disappearing all around the mansion—her precious Ming vase, the Lladro spaniel, the early Pollock. She was sure Dr. F was selling them to cover his overhead, his women, and his drugs, but she could play that game too. Starting with his Miura golf clubs. (She had briefly considered selling her breast milk online, something she had read about on the internet, but nixed that idea as "too messy." Plus, she'd have to get pregnant again to make that work, and she wasn't willing to risk the stretch marks and cellulite. She also wasn't sure she was willing to sleep with Dr. F unless he underwent the full gamut of STD tests—she had met a few of his nurses with whom she knew he had slept, and they looked like they belonged on a stripper pole, not in an operating room. Despite the fact that he occasionally tried to woo her into bed for old time's sake or during a husbandly renewal of affection, she always had a good excuse, usually involving a a graphic female problem that made Dr. F sputter and turn red and avoid her for the next two months, at least).

Those Muira golf clubs were what led her to Alexandra, who turned out to be a dream come true for an aging socialite who felt increasingly lost and alone. At Areli's (true) age (which not even her senile mother remembered, thank God), the water pills and laxatives were no longer effective enough for a quick fix to remedy the unsightly bulges in her newest couture outfits. Her husband had sucked her tiny frame within an inch of her life, and there was nowhere else to lipo. But Areli had recently found a great way to release all that stress and tension from running a huge household, reshape her body (non-surgically-what a concept), AND burn calories-Pilates. A new studio had just opened up in her neighborhood, and Areli and her few remaining friends, mainly women she had met at the gym post-Dottie, rushed to sign up for the exclusive $200-an-hour private lessons. The owner of the studio, Alexandra, was a former child star of the St. Petersburg Ballet. Unfortunately, Alexandra's knees and hips had long ago disintegrated. Steered to Pilates,where all the broken down ballerinas and gymnasts go, Alexandra had been immediately enthralled. It was the one place where she could still express herself to music, stay fit, and make dumpy suburban wives hate their bodies and envy hers. Damn it, but Alexandra had the sexiest lats, chest, and biceps Areli had ever seen. Knowing Alexandra's approximate real age made Pilates and the fabulous body all the more enticing. With close supervision and those extremely expensive "private" sessions, perhaps Areli could achieve the same results.

Selling the golf clubs to one of Dr. F's colleagues bought her the first ten lessons. By the end of them, her stomach was tight and her buns were higher than they had been in years—she couldn't believe it! Dr. F was starting to chase her around the bedroom again despite her excuses, and their yard worker had gotten a little handsy behind the hydrangeas (she feigned offense, but still made sure to give him a cash bonus in appreciation). Timmy, the delivery boy from Taco Tom's, even began dropping off complimentary beef enchiladas and often asked to come inside for a nice, cool glass of iced tea. Was Timmy lingering around for something more than just a little "sweet and low?" She couldn't tell, but she had to confess she enjoyed the attention from such an attractive young man with dark, dreamy eyes. And he looked even better from the back, as he cycled away! For the first time in years, she felt desirable. She felt like she was becoming a new woman--and it didn't even require a scalpel or a new wardrobe. For the first time in longer than she could remember, Areli had to confess that she had hoped for a different kind of life, instead of a blind allegiance to following the society status quo. She even began looking into how much becoming a trainer like Alexandra might cost, so that she could

bring this fabulous change into other women's lives as well. She had
given up her dream of being a children's PE teacher, but maybe her life
was meant to take a different path.

Of course, her fantasy only lasted until that fateful day when
the police showed up at her doorstep saying that her husband had
been taken to jail, and could they please take a look inside? She was
immediately offended and forbade them to enter—how dare they even
consider stepping foot inside her house? What if their shoes were
dirty? And no housekeeper to vacuum? And didn't they know it was
the height of rudeness to show up uninvited on a Tuesday afternoon?
They had a warrant, which certainly looked legal enough, and so after
asking them nicely to please put plastic wrap over their shoes, she let
them in.

New Arson, New Amie

When the police left, carrying several boxes of Dr. F's financial
files with them, Areli sank against the door, stunned. She had thought
losing her Neiman Marcus card was The Last Step on the Road to
Hell, but this—this was disastrous. And now they were on their way
to his office to do a second sweep there, gathering more damning
evidence of Dr. F's growing incompetence. Remembering that her
"before" pictures, taken in the most unflattering fluorescent light
and showing her at her dimpled, un-retouched worst, were at her
husband's office, she rushed over there on a mission to Seek and
Destroy. Finding the office deserted other than the receptionist, who
was painstakingly applying lip liner and fielding phone calls from the
press, Areli was stunned to discover that Esther had removed all the
files and checkbooks from the office, leaving behind a hastily scribbled
note reading: "See ya. Wouldn't want to be ya." Well, Areli would
have the last laugh with that—she knew for a fact that their checking
account had gone into the red just this morning with her purchase of
a new workout wardrobe, which fit into her Monday morning fitness

goals, and with Dr. F in jail there wouldn't be any income to replenish it. Esther couldn't spend what she didn't have.

Tearing up the office looking for unflattering photos of herself, as well as anything that might incriminate Dr. F and should certainly be destroyed, Areli stumbled across a female form, fast asleep with a darling little tabby in the surgery suite. Although Areli had not met Gabrielle before, she certainly recognized her husband's work. That sculpted stomach and wrinkle free neckline weren't created at the gym. All the noise startled Gabrielle and the cat, who screeched and leapt off the gurney.

Ever the charmer and unfailingly polite, even in the tensest of situations, Areli offered her hand to Gabrielle. "I'm Areli— Finkelstein. Dr. Finkelstein's wife. I can tell by your fabulous face and figure that you're a patient of my husband's, although he probably hasn't done any work on you lately, or you'd probably have a breast on your knee cap or a navel on your thigh. I swear he's been channeling Picasso—I can't even tell you the number of lawsuits pending against him right now—they could stack years onto his jail time if he's convicted in those proceedings, too. But enough about him. Do you have any idea where I can possibly find Esther White?"

Gabrielle, quite the talker herself, was unfazed by the rambling introduction. "I'm Gabrielle Issad. It is such a pleasure to finally meet you in person. Dr. F has told me so many wonderful things about you throughout the years—and of course I've seen your picture on his desk." She didn't mention that she had also seen a nurse bent over the aforenamed desk, her enhanced cleavage jiggling over a Finkelstein family photo from the Grand Canyon. That disclosure could be saved for another, more personal time. "Unfortunately, I can't tell you where Esther is, or Dr. Finkelstein, either, for that matter. There was no one here but the receptionist when I arrived. Do you think they're both OK? I was supposed to have a little brow freshener today, but I suppose I can reschedule—for a discount due to the inconvenience, of course."

Areli started to answer, but then her eyes caught a bright, shiny object wrapped daintily around Gabrielle's wrist—a vintage Patek Philippe. Areli had been dying for one just like it. Then she saw the time and gasped—she was late. "Listen, I have a Pilates class in twenty minutes. Would you care to join me, Gabrielle, and we can talk in the car? I can tell you that Dr. F probably won't be doing your surgery anytime soon—but this new workout can take years and inches off you, I swear."

They rushed out of the office, Areli clutching the only unflattering photograph of herself she could find (why on earth had that man framed a photograph of me when I was pregnant, she fussed to herself), which she would burn later. There was also the Christmas videotape from 1971 that they had sent out to all their patients years ago, with Dr. F dressed as Santa, Areli as an elf, and the tagline "Because Santa can't bring back the magic of your childhood Christmases, ask him for a facelift instead"—it would also have to be destroyed. It would be too easy for someone to figure out Areli's true age if they saw that video. Besides, they were Jewish, and the Christmas video might perplex her overseas relatives if it were released at the trial. (Not that anything on earth could embarrass them, but she didn't want to risk being cut out of any wills given the bleak turn in her fortune. Uncle Ben, the only Hassar with money left, always had been afraid that her move to the United States would encourage her to join Jews for Jesus, and he had threatened loudly and often that if that happened she wouldn't see a dime.)

Gabrielle didn't have any workout clothes with her (and now literally owned only the clothes on her back - a fact that would have horrified her younger self, but she deemed the loss of her fabulous designer wardrobe as well worth getting out of the Bad Adventures condos), but luckily Areli had a whole trunk full, the tags still on. They dropped the cat off at the McMansion and soon they were flopping around on their mats, their eyes fixed on Alexandra's perfect, muscular legs as she led them in the patented Pilates movements.

Muscles that Gabrielle didn't even know she had were screaming—this was amazing. If she had known about this when she was younger, she might not have required so much of Dr. F's assistance. She needed to think fast, though—Areli would want to drop her off somewhere, and Gabrielle didn't know if she could manage to sneak back into Dr. F's office, where she could crash until she developed a firm plan for her uncertain future.

"Do you want to grab lunch?" Gabrielle asked, trying to sweat as prettily as she could—she hadn't exerted herself this much in years, even in bed. "There's a little Italian place around the corner—I think a workout like that deserves a glass of wine."

"Sure," Areli said, shrugging. "My husband's in prison. I might as well drink. I took the only company card that Esther missed—we'll expense it."

They settled in at a patio table and ordered a glass of wine and two bowls of minestrone soup--no solid food, of course. They sipped the broth, ignoring the vegetables in the bowl. The warm, fresh garlic bread sticks did make Areli's eyes tear up when she looked at them—though it had been years since she'd enjoyed carbs, she still remembered them fondly and regretted that she hadn't spent more time with them—much like the feeling one has after losing a beloved family member. Gabrielle, thinking Areli was emotional from the recent trauma of losing a husband to the penal system, patted her fine, thin shoulder in sympathy.

The wine loosened their lips, and the two women, both now adrift in the world, were soon sharing their darkest secrets. Gabrielle told Areli about her traumatizing (and yet, still thrilling) experience at an American Indian Pow Wow in Ponca City, Oklahoma, and Areli told Gabrielle about her sexual fantasies involving Timmy and his strong, young, muscular body. She even told Gabrielle about a clandestine kiss one afternoon when Timmy had delivered their new antique English wall tapestry.

"I knew I shouldn't have," Areli said sorrowfully. "I knew it was wrong. I'm married, and I made a vow to be loyal to Dr. F—but I've suspected for years that he's sleeping with every nurse and patient he has, in addition to that awful Judy Gibran. But the kiss—I can't even describe it. I fantasized about him for years when he delivered all those high fat, high carb terrible meals from Taco Tom's. I ordered them just to see him, and then I threw them away. And then he got his license and started delivering for Neiman's, and you should have seen his bis and tris flex when he picked up a package. And he was so polite about the kiss. He even apologized for taking advantage of me. If only I had met a man like him when I was young—things might have turned out differently."

"If you hadn't married Dr. F, you'd be a saggy fright," said Gabrielle honestly. "If I could do it over again, I'd marry a plastic surgeon. You got for free what I've paid thousands for. Besides, my husband left me for a fat Greek donkey named Elena, whom he met on a cruise. She had a moustache and cellulite, but it was true love. I hope they're happy. I also hope they fell over the edge of that boat and drowned. At least they don't have anywhere to come home to. I took care of that. Of course, now I don't have anywhere to go, either."

Areli wrinkled her brow, as best she could. "What do you mean? Why can't you go home? Did he already have the locks changed, like with poor Edie Anderson? She came home one day and there was already another woman in their house--wearing her clothes, which were a size too large, to add insult to injury. Her husband had filed for divorce and kicked her out without even telling her."

Gabrielle poured herself another big glass of wine and took a gulp. "George Foreman grill caught fire," she choked out. "Freak accident. Burned down my whole building. Luckily, no one was inside—but I lost everything. All I have now are these clothes and my cat." The stark reality of this hit her hard. Her eyes welled up with real tears, for once. This was not ever where she dreamed she would end up when she was a girl in Gravestone. But then as this glimmer of a tear slid down her perfect, small nose, Gabrielle felt her mood rise a little, remembering the Lebanese hooked beak she had inherited. Things weren't all bad. She was homeless, but at least she looked good.

Areli put her hand over Gabrielle's. "I am so sorry, Gabrielle. That sounds terrible—you can stay with me until the insurance money comes and you get back on your feet." It was such a relief to have someone to talk to—someone who seemed to listen to her and care. And if Gabrielle stayed with her for a while, she wouldn't have to be all alone in that big house. She was more than a little lonely after her youngest child had left for college, and Dr. F's sudden departure, as she euphemistically thought of it. Maybe Gabrielle could cook for her? Then again, maybe not so much. Just from looking at Gabrielle, she doubted it—those perfectly manicured nails had probably never touched a pan, unless it was to throw it at the maid.

As they continued to sip their wine and admired each other's Body by Finkelstein work, they began a beautiful friendship. Oh, sure, Areli didn't like it that Gabrielle had been such a good friend of Judy's. But Judy was out of the way now, due to circumstances that Areli had to sadly admit were unfortunate (though, karmically appropriate).

Areli became increasingly excited as she thought of more and more things she and Gabrielle could do together. It would be like having the sister and best friend she never had. "We can purchase a duet package at River Stokes Pilates Studio." Areli added. "That saves so much money, and we'll have to be frugal now after all that's happened. You can even take Dr. F's Benz to work if you want to. The doors are a little dinged up, but other than that it's still a nice car."

"Oh, I have my car," Gabrielle said. "I left it at Dr. F's office. But I'll still drive his—see if we can add a few more dents to it. A little payback for when he gets released. I'm an expert at backing into poles and hitting curbs—it used to drive Salaam insane."

An admiring gentleman at the next table offered to pay their bill, but the girls insisted on paying their own way. They drove back to

River Stokes, cozying up with another bottle of wine in front of the fake fireplace, sharing their life stories. And after that they were inseparable. They put on their makeup together in the morning, went for jogs at the same time, and even sat side by side for internet shopping (Areli had now been banned from everywhere in the Gallermaria except Aunt Annie's pretzels, the only place she didn't owe money). Both terrified of and excited about the future, they dreamed of what their new lives would become and they worked on shedding the painful memories of the past through long, wine-soaked conversations and by calling Ms. Chloe, Houston's famed astrologer. They were bonded by their love of fashion, a lingering loyalty to Dr. F and a respect for his talent in his earlier years, and an enthusiasm for Pilates. And most serendipitously of all, it turned out that Areli's Uncle Ben's village in Israel was just across the border from the home town of many of Gabrielle's Lebanese relatives, where they had a convenience store that trafficked heavily in Scotch and cigarettes. What a small world!

Funeral of the Century

Despite their budding friendship, Gabrielle couldn't convince Areli to pay her last respects to Judy (perhaps because Areli had no respect for Judy to begin with). So, Gabrielle went to say goodbye to her old friend on her own. And Judy's funeral was just what everyone would have expected from her: flashy, trashy, and crassy. Queen Nefertiti's funeral procession probably paled in comparison. The over-the-top slide show featuring Judy and her doggie, Francisco, wearing "mother/son" matching outfits, Power Shopping at the Gallamaria, and enjoying a candlelit dinner at the Five Seasons Hotel, where Francisco had his own little puppy dog tray of heart-healthy snacks, served by white gloved waiters, was all too touching.

The funeral featured black-tied waiters in top hats, feather boas, and assless chaps. Yes, it might have been a little less than hygienic to have them carrying about the trays of crab quiche, but no one in attendance complained, and more than one of the guests snuck in a little pinch of those fine, firm, flexing buttocks. Beautiful semi-nude boys and girls performed Cirque du Soleil-like acrobatics, adding a strange sexual charge to such a somber occasion. Judy's favorite platform shoes, furs and outfits were displayed on live (mostly female) models, who also passed around trays of champagne and hors d'oeuvres. It was truly The Funeral of the Century. Judy could still draw a crowd, even if some of the guests were simply vultures, hoping to make business contacts in order to scoop up the remains of her real estate empire. All of her best friends were there, however--Ike and Darren sat in the front row, their hats draped with fabulous crepe veils discreetly trimmed with Swarovski crystals. Gabrielle sat snugly between them, dressed in a brilliant pink mini-dress and matching hankie. (Judy wouldn't have wanted black. Nor would she ever actually expect Gabrielle to use the thoughtful, matching pink hankie and mess up her make-up). Even a somber Bubba Longview had come, dressed in a stiff black suit and remembering with sad nostalgia Judy's youthful glow (thanks, La Mer!) and jiggling bosom on that day when she had driven up in her custom luxury automobile into the dusty, graveled lot of his radio station. After three short sermons by Judy's childhood priest, her feng shui master, and astrologer, Ms. Cleo, the viewing began as a four-string quartet softly played their versions of "Hot Stuff," "Brick House," and "Love to Love You, Baby" in the background. As Judy's casket was brought forward through the crowd, hoisted upon the shoulders of six Nubian slaves (well, OK--she had to settle for six former drug dealers from Colombia, Mexico, and Guatemala--but they were still quite the spectacle: tanned, barefoot, and wearing flashy sequined shirts and white linen pants. Plus, she had to have someone strong enough to carry her heavy mahogany coffin--even though the tags on her chic black dress said "2," she was oddly heavy).

The funeral party then solemnly gathered round for more drinks and complimentary astrology readings by Ms. Chloe, who gratefully accepted the generous cash tips from the sad mourners. The little sign she had printed reading "Help Me - Help Francisco's Future" insured that the guests would empty their pockets. Thank goodness this aging crowd was helpless without their reading glasses.

After several glasses of champagne, Gabrielle discreetly slipped dear Francisco, wearing his custom made diamond bumble bee dog collar, designed by Judy, into her Hermes Kelly bag, along with a couple of extra hand-crafted artisan chocolates which bore Judy's pink, swoopy company logo, "for the road." (Chocolate was vegetarian, and, like Grey Goose, therefore, healthy.) Francisco would need a new home, and Gabrielle had all the love to give him now that Judy's premature demise had left a huge hole in her shallow little heart.

Orange is Not the New Black

In the excitement of acquiring a two new pets as well as a new Best Friend Forever, Gabrielle had completely forgotten about the Bad Adventures incident. Plus, that had been weeks ago--it was ancient news. She was sure she couldn't get in trouble for the fire anymore even if she did get caught. There had to be some sort of time limit on criminal liability, right? And the streets were full of murderers and crack addicts—the truly dangerous. The police would do well to focus on those desperate souls and not go after someone who had merely been doing what was basically community service. Besides, those toxic fumes from the building practically made it self-defense.

Asleep in Dr. F's fine Italian linens, still recovering from an intense Pilates workout, Gabrielle was awakened by a panicked Areli. Those awful, sweaty, poorly dressed policemen with their dirty shoes were at the door again, this time asking for Gabrielle. They had been tracking her for weeks. Fortunately, they already knew to put plastic on their shoes before entering the Finkelstein McMansion and had brought shower caps from the jail just for that purpose. At least Areli had made an impression on them the last time they were here. In appreciation, perhaps she would offer them tea? If only she could find her china....

Areli stood at the door broken hearted as she lost yet another loved one to the cruel hands of the law. Gabrielle tried every trick in the book to weasel her way out of this uncomfortable predicament: acting like a flirt, a bitch, a victim, a super salesperson - even a pathetic, lame attempt to show them her full body wax...but the cops wouldn't let her out of the mess. She was charged with arson, willful destruction of property, and attempted murder. Poor thing didn't even get a strip search at the jail house. When they finally got her behind bars, Gabrielle took one look around and began screaming: "Get me out of here with these fucking losers!" The other inmates and even some of the jailers were too afraid to go near Gabrielle, because they thought she was insane and would have made a better inmate in the psychiatric ward. And, at this point, they weren't far wrong—her nails were chipped, she needed a straightener, and she hadn't even done anything wrong. People *could* have been in the building, but they hadn't been; and she was sure that if the police would just ask the residents of Bad Adventures they would hail Gabrielle as their savior, leading them from the hellish nightmare of diminishing property values. She had always known that justice was blind, but apparently she was a bitch, too.

Gabrielle languished in prison for what seemed like years, without even a nail file—her cuticles were soon as ragged as her nerves, and her roots were beginning to show. And because there was no spa at the jail, she had no way to receive her full body massages. She had tried to contact Salaam, hoping to get a favor for old time's sake, but that saggy assed Elena answered his cell phone instead.

"Help you get a lawyer?" she said snottily. "I'm sure Salaam has no interest in helping you do anything, after you broke his heart, spent all his money, and burned down his home. Besides, we don't have any money to spare--we're moving to a penthouse downtown, with an extra room for Mrs. Abdullah. We get along so well. She tells me she's finally gotten the daughter she always wanted. Mrs. Abdullah is teaching me to make authentic hummus from her very own family recipe. She said your chick peas were absolutely STALE."

Gabrielle slammed the public phone down into the cradle so violently that she broke a nail. She regretted giving Dr. F's business card to that hairy little harlot now. Why, they had practically shared a husband and they were almost related. And without Salaam's help she certainly couldn't afford the top-notch lawyer that she needed in order to get out of this mess without more jail time and permanent mortification.

She had only been in prison for two months, but it was the longest two months of her life—and it made the dusty streets of Gravestone look like Ibiza. How could she ever look attractive in flats and traffic cone orange loose garments that made her skin sallow and her teeth yellow. It simply was not fair! And the necessities were the bare minimum and wholly unacceptable--all she wanted was whitening strips for her teeth and a bar of Fragonard soap--was that too much to ask? Gabrielle was getting ready to make a pact with Goldman Sachs or God or Buddha or Zeus or *somebody* to move back to Gravestone and take care of her parents if only she were released—but luckily Timmy's killer legal skills saved the day before that horrible thought entered the universe a second time.

When Areli told him about Gabrielle's plight, Timmy talked one of his colleagues into transferring her case to him. By arguing that the popcorn ceilings at the Bad Adventures contained asbestos that had caused her to suffer temporary dementia, he was able to get her a deferred sentence with three years probation (although Gabrielle had secretly been hoping for a Really Well Hung Jury). Gabrielle would have to meet with her probation officer once a month and attend mandatory therapy once a week for a year. Though to her disappointment her probation officer wasn't the hunky, muscled civil servant worthy of a male pin-up calendar she had dreamed of, she did enjoy the counseling—it felt great to get all of her innermost secrets and disappointments out in the open. She began to secretly suspect that it might ultimately make her happier than alcohol and drugs (though it wasn't remotely as much fun).

Gabrielle was released immediately after her trial, and she couldn't wait to get back to her life with Areli and the cat, to whom she had become quite attached and had named Tabitha. Francisco, the chihuahua of the late, great Judy Gibran, had been quite good-natured about the cat, and, with a mutual interest in snacking between meals, they had become fast friends. Making it back to the McMansion just in time for a Pilates class with Areli (whew! She really needed a professional workout), Gabrielle was puzzled to see Areli crying. She had just been served with divorce papers from Dr. F, who had been released early from prison for good behavior three weeks ago, but hadn't seen fit to even call his anxious, waiting wife. Areli couldn't believe it. Although she had known in her heart that things between the two of them had not been going well for years, he was still the father of her children. She had pictured them growing old together, taking the grandchildren on family vacations, and most of all BASKING in the countless luxuries cash brings. (Surely nothing had happened to that secret bank account he held in Liechtenstein?) Yes, she had been considering leaving him and she was sick to death of his cheating and habitual morning spraying of the mirror with toothpaste droplets, but she had hoped maybe they could get help—perhaps couples counseling or even a marital retreat. But to be left first—Areli, who was used to being loved and pampered—she couldn't wrap her head around it. The last two months had been so hard—without Gabrielle, without Dr. F, and this was the final straw.

But the worst day of Areli's life wasn't over quite yet. Timmy, who had brought by a bag of bean burritos for old time's sake, and to welcome Gabrielle home, gently sat Areli down to share some very shocking news with her. It turns out that Esther White's son, Neal, had actually been fathered by Dr. F. Timmy had always been suspicious of that sneaky Esther, and he had smuggled a lock of Neal's hair years ago when he was delivering summonses for the DA's office.

Under the guise of admiring Neal's artfully placed highlights, Timmy had managed to snatch a few strands. And, of course, it was easy to get a sample of Esther's saliva from the flask she always kept hidden in her desk drawer. Timmy was able to match their DNA, proving just what he and others in the office had always suspected. At this news, Areli was absolutely devastated. She wondered if Dr. F had known about his illegitimate son, and if their affair had lasted longer than a couple of nicely brewed Long Island Iced Teas. How could that woman have looked her in the eye for all these years, knowing that she was a homewrecker. No wonder she had endured so many complimentary surgeries from Dr. F. Then Areli found the bright side--at least now she had an iron-clad connection to the annual Barney's sample sale. Neal couldn't keep his own stepmother out, and as a recent divorcee with a questionable source of alimony, she couldn't keep buying full retail price like she had before. She had taken those magical boxes filled with sample sizes for granted before, but no longer.

As a final blow, however, Timmy handed over a tender, touching goodbye letter from Dr. F, who revealed that he had met and fallen in love with Shacronda, one of the black female prison guards, and he hoped that they could all someday be friends. He included a picture of the two of them in Vegas, Shacronda's grills gleaming and her fleshy body straining the seams of her sequined mini-dress. Areli just didn't understand—she already had the perfect body, and Dr. F wasn't allowed to practice plastic surgery anymore—so why would he choose a fixer-upper like Shacronda? (She would later learn that Dr. F's love of golf had come into play, and it turned out that Shacondra had a mean grip on the putter.)

Gabrielle forced Areli to put on her cutest tights and threw her into the car. A hearty workout, followed by the usual drinks and maybe a little arm wrestling with Alexandra, would take Areli's mind off things. Gabrielle had realized in prison that Judy's words so long ago were right—think like a man, but act like a woman. But one of the few things Judy hadn't taught her was that you need great friends; and thanks to Areli, Gabrielle had figured out that one on her own.

Old World, New World

Alexandra, upon seeing Areli's stricken face as she stumbled through the Pilates studio door, immediately opened a bottle of vodka and poured them all a big glass. She then rushed out all her other customers and threw the deadbolt, flipping the shop sign to "Closed."

"Ah, you be okay," she said in her thick Russian accent as she came back over to Areli, who was sitting weakly on a mat. "You drink, you feel better until you fall asleep. You wake up, feel worse, drink more. Eventually you forget why you so sad."

"My life has fallen apart," sniffled Areli. "I don't think drinking will help. Nothing will help. I don't know what to do."

"Is not such bad tragedy, this" Alexandra insisted, waving her glass around emphatically. "Take Alexandra. When I was young, I was BEAUTIFUL. Most beautiful ballerina in Russia. Body like a stick, perfect for dancing Swan Lake. I was in magazines, newspapers— everyone love me. Then, my knees go bad. Too much strain over the years. I was washed up, nobody. But then, I move to America, land of opportunity. I try working in restaurant, not making enough. I try running dry cleaner, not making enough. Korean corner markets, no room for Alexandra. Then I start Pilates. Now it's national chain, one in every big city. Now, I have plenty of money. In fact, here, I give you some." Alexandra reached into her faux Faberge egg and handed Areli a roll of worthless Russian rubles, circa 1988. "You buy new outfit, feel better. And soon I achieve my most favorite dream—Pilates in Paris. Can you imagine Alexandra, living in Paris? The French, they love pain, they will love my Pilates class. I will stretch their stiff snobby spines in ways you only see in French cinema."

Gabrielle and Areli's eyes lit up—they saw their chance to finally get out and make a new start. Areli had never had a job, other than wife and mother, both of which had been stressful- often figure sacrificing and time-consuming. But now those days were over. With all the distractions of having to feed Tabitha and walk Francisco, as well as her awful trial and subsequent jail time, Gabrielle had completely forgotten about her job at the radio station, and they had replaced her with a twenty-two-year-old with big boobs. Natural ones. So far. Gabrielle hadn't been too offended. Trixie seemed like a very nice girl (although not nearly enough of a barracuda to survive in the brutal world of radio sales where amateurs were a dime a dozen). Gabrielle was secure in knowing that no one in the wild world of radio sales could ever compare to her track record.

The next day, they stormed into the bookstore and bought a pile of French grammar books, a Business for Dummies book, and two low-fat mochas to get started on their new path. Areli had already begun her certification process to become a Pilates instructor, but had lacked the funds to finish. While she had made a small profit off Dr. F's collection of jeweled cuff links, it hadn't been quite enough to pay all the bills *and* take the final two classes on advanced Pilates instruction. But Areli was willing to be patient. Finally, she was taking charge of her own life and making steps toward becoming the kind of strong capable woman she had always admired. It felt great.

Now, if she could find a way to complete the expensive certification process perhaps they really could open the Paris studio! And she was sure now that Alexandra would help them financially— they could all go to Paris together. Under Areli's positive influence, the New Gabrielle had sworn off drugs, hard liquor and carbs. Her superbly sharp selling and marketing skills, honed from years in radio sales, re-emerged and she would build up the Pilates clientele—especially since Gabrielle had been practicing her French for years in anticipation of eventually becoming a Parisian. The women were giddy with excitement at the prospect of beginning a different life, a different dream, in a different location.

Unfortunately, though, Alexandra had to confess that she didn't have quite enough saved to start the studio—the business permits, rent, work visas and other particulars all added up to a truly daunting amount of money. Areli decided to keep her latest Oriental rug—it would look great in the Paris studio. Judy's estate sale had also proved to be a treasure trove of discounted artifacts to class up their new studio. Areli's next plan was to sell the house—but it was in Dr. F's name, and when she contacted his lawyer to ask about the sale, he firmly informed her that Dr. F would be bringing his blushing bride, Shacronda, to the McMansion where they would live and start a new family in the near future. However, perhaps she would like Dr. F's Miura golf clubs, as he had a new set now?

Areli and Gabrielle racked their brains for where could they get the rest of the funds they needed to get started, but it wasn't until one day in Neiman's (just browsing, of course) that the light from within Areli's soul relocated to her now sensible, scheming head: *Esther*. Areli knew that Esther had been cooking the books at Dr. Finkelstein's Facelifts, Facials, and More! Center for years—there was no way she could have lived the lifestyle she enjoyed on her salary from Dr. F, especially after she ditched her oil baron husband. Nobody who worked as a glorified receptionist could afford Prada and Dolce and Gabbana on such a regular basis. They had to find her and blackmail her for some of that money back. Her brain quickly scanned for inspiration from episodes of "Monk".

After a quick Internet search, Gabrielle and Areli discovered Esther's new home address in Spring, Texas, outside of Houston.

The exhausting hour-long drive to Spring (which found them exiting forbidden highway stops at such establishments as Cookie Cabin and Flapjacks Frenzy) had lead to a dead end. Upon arrival, the girls saw the home address listed on the Internet was an uninhabited trailer with pink flamingos on the lawn. WHERE could Esther be? Following their feminine instincts, they hightailed it to the nearest country club, where they immediately spotted her fondling a twenty-something caddy, knocking back a dirty martini and wearing an emerald cocktail ring the size of a small planet—her retirement present to herself.

"Put down that cocktail right now," demanded Areli, in the most aggressive voice she had used in years. The last time she had used that mean voice was when she was fourteen years old and had demanded that the servants match her purse to her shoes. That guava juice at the Flapjacks Frenzy House fifteen minutes up the highway was really working its magic now

Esther, choking, on an olive, whirled around, wiping dry martini off her chin. Her eyes widened. "Areli!" she gasped. "What are you doing here?"

"Timmy Ranger, *attorney at law,* was suspicious of you from the beginning. Who in their right mind would refuse complimentary fajitas from Taco Tom's, especially when Timmy is 'delivering'? Plus he always sensed your suppressed resentment toward his idol, Dr. F. Furthermore, one of the checks you gave him bounced, and he recognized the signature as fraudulent. YOUR fraud. We have those—Gabrielle, what are they called?"

Gabrielle asserted, "*Surveillance* tapes!"

Areli continued, picking up steam and confidence. "Yes, surveillance tapes! Not only did Timmy hire a private dick to watch your sorry, sagging ass, Esther So-Called "WHITE," but he also obtained several different security videos showing you walking out of the Finkelstein Facelifts, Facials and More! Center with checkbooks and files tucked under your flabby arms. Money bags that you never

128

took to the bank to deposit like you were supposed to. Furthermore, Timmy took saliva samples from your office "coffee" cup and matched them with a hair sample from your son, Neal. We all know for sure that Neal is really the son of Dr. F. If you don't give us $2 million dollars right now, we are going to the FBI or the CIA or something with the tapes. You'll be behind bars faster than you can do a poorly extended high-kick, you stealing tramp."

Esther was totally taken aback. She didn't want to give them any money—but she also didn't want to go to jail or have to tell Neal who his real father was. He already had enough identity issues. "OK. Fine, girls. You win—at least this round. Follow me to my locker in the gym. I have enough cash in my sports bra to shut you two bitches up for a long time." There wasn't anywhere near $2 million in Esther's locker, but there was more than enough to jump start their business—Areli confiscated Esther's ring and Gabrielle grabbed her Jimmy Choos, too. She would just have to slink home barefoot and accessory-less—in shame, getting just what she deserved.

It's a Long Way to the Top If You Want to Rock 'n' Roll

Gabrielle and Areli had their first-class seats to Paris booked the next day, and they sprang for Alexandra's seat too. After all, she was the one opening the studio for them to run. Adding to the merriment was their discovery that their trendy Left Bank Pilates studio was housed next door to a Plastic Surgeon's office. Not only would the girls have new clothing shops to experience, but a new shop for their nip/tucks--or at least a little lunchtime Juvederm refresher. The cosmetic surgery laws weren't as strict in Europe, meaning that they could receive cutting edge procedures (so to speak) sooner than anyone else.

With Timmy's help they cut through all the red tape involved in opening a franchise overseas. It seems there were some immigration problems with Alexandra's citizenship, and perhaps she had NOT really been a Russian ballerina after all, and perhaps her actual birth name was ALEX (that would explain her broad shoulders, Adam's apple, and perfect six-pack, at least), but those problems were quickly resolved and soon they were all en route to the City of Light. The first class seats were amazing, roomy, and plush, and they were soon giddy on the complimentary champagne. Areli, living on the edge for once, even had a cookie and didn't instantly regret it--even if she did pick out the chocolate chips and discreetly hide them in her napkin.

As the pretty but slightly chubby Air Paris HostTitute stopped by to refill their champagne glasses, Gabrielle was struck with nostalgia. Standing before her was herself, twenty years ago. The extra weight in the hips, the prominent Semitic Lebanese nose, the ample, untouched cleavage that would desperately need a lift in 5+ years. Grabbing the young girl by the arm, she whispered: "Kitten! You'd be such a beautiful girl if you could only drop a few pounds and get that nose fixed!"

The stewardess smacked the glass down in front of Gabrielle. "You're one to talk--your nose is perfect. Why do you think I'm working this shitty job? It's not for long, though--soon I'll have enough saved to get a rhinoplasty, and then I'm going to be a famous actress. And at least being a stewardess got me out of that podunk Kentucky town I was born in."

Gabrielle smiled in recognition--perhaps this girl needed a mentor. Gabrielle slipped her a business card, with her name and the new Pilates studio address embossed on the front in swoopy gold lettering. "If you're ever in Paris, look me up," she said. "I think we'd have a lot to talk about. And this workout class will whip you into such shape you can go a good three more years without lipo."

As Gabrielle, Areli, and Alexandra toasted each other (no room to arm wrestle on the plane), the pilot mentioned that if you looked out the left side of the plane, you could see the flat land of Oklahoma. Okla-fricking-homa-less! That seemed like such a long time ago--but not too long ago for Gabrielle to remember the taunts from the flabby, toothless hillbillies years ago. Assy Issad, indeed! In a gesture of sisterly solidarity, all three girls stood up and, with their taut Pilates asses, mooned the red dust state. The words of the immortal Uncle Ben came to mind: "TILHOUS TEEZI! LICK MY ASSHOLE!"

Epilogue

Gabrielle, Areli and Alexandra had been living in Paris for several weeks, preparing for their grand opening and getting settled into their new flat. They already had a growing client list--Gabrielle's sales skills and Alexandra's strikingly ripped abs and low body fat had served them in good stead. As their limo arrived at Areli's House of Pilates, Facials, and More! Studio for the big Opening Day Red Carpet Kick Off, the girls were stunned to see Ike, Darrin, and Neal standing in front of the building, holding armloads of roses and champagne. It seems they had sneaked into town a few days earlier in order to properly decorate the studio for the girls, who had left the old tenant's cliched Eiffel Tower decoration scheme largely in place. They knew they could not count on Areli or Gabrielle to use a hammer and nail, so they had taken it upon themselves to insure a proper Paris welcome for the new business endeavor. (You might not think Ike and Darrin would be able to use a hammer or nail either, of course, as their favorite tools were now eyelash curlers, but Ike's father had frequently insisted that Ike put down the purse and pick up a power sander in his youth.) With uncharacteristic restraint, the boys had taken it easy on their usual rainbow motif and instead had gone for a subtle Armani-inspired earth tone decor.

After a celebratory kir royale toast, they all settled into the brown leather chairs in the studio to wait for their first clients. A loud bark disturbed their brief tranquility. As Francisco ran to the front door, and Tabitha hissed viciously, Areli and Gabrielle ran to the large bay window that fronted the studio and peered out with suspicion. To their surprise, a large black woman with grills was hoisting herself out of a limo, followed by a large white standard poodle, and--could it possibly be?--Dr. Finkelstein followed by Dr. Tripp. It seems that even though they were not allowed to practice medicine in the U.S., the growing French appetite for plastic surgery was booming, and they were welcomed with open arms. They had taken their French boards and had leased the space next door! What a small world!

Finkelstein's Facelifts a la Carte! proved to be a profitable endeavor and reminded Dr. F of his glory days of old back in Houston. Curly, Dr. Tripp's friend from prison, really had a knack for details and had a surprising command of the female form. Curly's post-op cosmetic makeovers proved a huge hit, and he was truly an artist at hiding those unsightly post-face-lift bruises.

Areli's studio flourished as well, with Gabrielle's marketing and selling skills creating a huge demand on the Pilates classes. True to form, Gabrielle hired some amazing instructors. Tartain, a former aerobics instructor, and Fatima, a former Tunisian belly dancer, were taken back a bit by the rigorous, in depth interviewing process conducted personally by Gabrielle. Though they thought the professional level strip search was unorthodox, they were thrilled just to be associated with Areli's publicity rich new studio.

What could possibly go wrong?

Made in the USA .
Coppell, TX
28 October 2019